"I've got some news tha
to you, Dare."

She sat up, frowning. "Are

"Yes."

"Don't tell me they're sending me back to the States, Ram. I won't go. My place is here."

He gave her a pained look and held out the paper to her. "I have no say in this. Read it."

She reached for the extended paper, her fingertips brushing his. The ache in her heart for this man, who was incredibly closed up, remained an enigma to her.

His eyes darkened and he looked away for a moment, his mouth tightening.

"I'm being ordered back into your team? As your combat field medic?" She stared at the orders and then drilled a look into his unhappy-looking gaze. "These are legit? Seriously, Ram?"

"I wish it was a joke," he answered heavily, pushing his fingers through his short dark hair after taking off his cap. "It's for real, Dare."

NO TURNING BACK

New York Times **Bestselling Author**

LINDSAY McKENNA

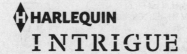

To the wonderful, courageous people of Ukraine, who are so very brave, resilient and tenacious, who fiercely defend their freedom and their country. Having served in the military, I support your fight for continued democracy. Just know that the people of the USA are behind you 100 percent. We hold the people of Ukraine in our hearts.

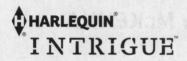

Recycling programs for this product may not exist in your area.

ISBN-13: 978-1-335-59162-3

No Turning Back

Copyright © 2024 by Nauman Living Trust

Harlequin Enterprises ULC
22 Adelaide St. West, 41st Floor
Toronto, Ontario M5H 4E3, Canada
www.Harlequin.com

Printed in Lithuania

MIX
Paper | Supporting responsible forestry
FSC® C021394

Lindsay McKenna is proud to have served her country in the US Navy as an aerographer's mate third class—also known as a weather forecaster. She was a pioneer in the military romance subgenre and loves to combine heart-pounding action with soulful and poignant romance. True to her military roots, she is the originator of the long-running and reader-favorite Morgan's Mercenaries series. She does extensive hands-on research, including flying in aircraft such as a P3-B Orion sub-hunter and a B-52 bomber. She was the first romance writer to sign her books in the Pentagon bookstore. Visit her online at lindsaymckenna.com.

Books by Lindsay McKenna

Harlequin Intrigue

No Turning Back

HQN Books

The Wyoming Series

Out Rider
Night Hawk
Wolf Haven
High Country Rebel
The Loner
The Defender

Visit the Author Profile page at
Harlequin.com for more titles.

CAST OF CHARACTERS

Sergeant Dare Mazur—A US Army Special Forces advanced combat field medic, she's on military loan to the Ukrainian Army to teach their combat medics advanced field surgery skills in order to save more lives on the battlefield.

Captain Ram Kozak—Black ops team leader in the Ukrainian Army, Black Wolf Regiment. The last person he expected to see again was Dare Mazur, in Kyiv. He'd lost touch with her for two years and now his unspoken love for her is going to be tested once again. He's an officer and she's enlisted. There can be no fraternization and she has unexpectedly been assigned to his unit.

Sergeant Adam Vorona—Second-in-command of the black ops team in the Ukrainian Army, Black Wolf Regiment, and like a brother to Dare Mazur. He's delighted she will return to her old team to be with them once again.

Lera Vorona—Wife to Sergeant Adam Vorona. She is a dynamo with two adorable young daughters. The friendship between her and Dare is sisterly, and the entire family loves having Dare spend her weekends with them.

Chapter One

November 1, 2021

Captain Ram Kozak was in a quagmire of emotions. On a cold, windy day, he took the steps out of the Ukrainian Army Headquarters in Kyiv. The sky was swollen and pregnant with dark and light gray clouds hanging over the sprawling, beautiful capital. In his hand he clutched a set of orders and that was what made his heart ache. As he climbed concrete steps up to the educational facility part of the massive complex, a shred of hope filtered through him, and the roiling in his gut temporarily subsided.

He was going to see Sergeant Darina Mazur, a US Army Special Forces combat medic on loan to the Ukrainian Army. She was teaching, he'd found out only earlier in the morning, advanced combat field surgery to Ukrainian Army medics. They needed this specialized training because the US Special Forces school was located in the USA and right now, it wasn't feasible for their medics to attend it half a world away. The news that Dare Mazur was the instructor hit him like a powerful emotional earthquake. He did his best to hide the shock as his colonel, who headed up SSO Third Special Purpose Regiment, their ops group known as the Black Wolf Brigade, hurried to meet the Russian threat coming in February 2022. The orders he'd been given were special, that Sgt. Mazur, an experienced field surgeon and combat medic, who had advanced lifesaving skills, would be taken out of the classroom and placed back into his team once more.

He slid his key code card into the slot, and his brown brows fell as he pulled open the thick bulletproof glass door and entered. Well-known for his poker face, Ram was sure his boss saw the shock in his eyes, if only momentarily. Four years earlier, his team had been in Afghanistan, on the front lines, at a top-secret US camp near the Pakistan border. Dare had been their combat medic, going out on every team mission with them, risking her life. She had been assigned to his team because their medic's tour was up and they needed a replacement. Ram wasn't against women in combat. Almost a fifth of the Ukrainian Army consisted of women in every specialty, including combat and some of them being field medics.

At twenty-five, he'd not been prepared for the easygoing, smiling U.S. Special Forces woman. Everyone called her Dare, and in the two years she spent with his team in Afghanistan, she certainly earned her nickname. Whatever hesitancy he had about the American woman dissolved. She might save lives, but she could take them, too, when it came to their mutual enemy, the Taliban and ISIS fighters. She was also cross-trained as a sniper, a backup to the two male snipers who were already on his team.

What he hadn't counted on was his falling in love with her. *That* was a shock to his system. How to remain her commanding officer and never reveal his need to share a personal relationship with her, whether on a mission, at the US camp or aiding her medical efforts to help the Afghan people of the surrounding villages. She was calm under fire. Her specialty, her gift, was her healing abilities, he'd discovered. It didn't matter if it was a camp dog with a bloodied paw, a child with a hurt finger or one of the elderly from nearby villages who needed her medical skills. She was present and accounted for. There was nothing he could dislike about her. Compassion wasn't his thing, but it was hers. Maybe it was her femininity, her softness and gentle nature instead of that testosterone team she was part of, that soothed the inner edges of himself, as well as the rest of his aggressive black ops team. He couldn't really define or quantify it, but Dare's presence was a gift.

Before he'd met her, his gut was always a churning, angry snake in the pit of his stomach when out on an op. He worried about every member of his team. He'd lost his entire family at age eighteen, and he'd adopted his team in the military as his pseudo-family, without consciously thinking about it. The team members were like brothers to him, tightly knit and close. When Dare came into the team, she was immediately absorbed by all of them in the best of ways, but he, as their officer and leader, had to remain remote and unemotional toward her, which was the last thing he wanted to do or be.

Grappling with his memories, he went inside the warm building, the waxed and shining sand-colored tile floor beneath his polished combat boots. He decided to take the stairwell to the third floor, where all the classrooms were located, slowing down, hesitant to meet her once again. The two years they'd been apart, she was given orders to come to Lviv, to teach advanced combat medicine to their Ukrainian Army medics. He thought with time and distance, his ache for her would dissolve. But it had not.

Dare had a minor in botany and loved flowers. The team would purposely keep an eye out for any poor, struggling, thirsty plant when out on an op, and give it to her. She could always identify it and she would smile with delight, her light blue eyes sparkling with joy, as she gently cradled the plant in her hands. She melted his tough outer walls that protected him from the emotions of everyday life. Somehow, she'd gotten through his shield and had gently held his vulnerable inner core that he'd never allowed anyone to get near. But she had. Maybe that's why he fell in love with her. Had she earned his trust? Ram didn't know and savagely stuffed all his fanciful wonderings back deep down inside himself. It had nothing to do with what was about to happen.

He hadn't solved or resolved his lovelorn situation regarding Dare after she received orders to leave his team and Afghanistan. Not wanting to lose touch with her, he continued to take photos with his smartphone during ops of any flowers he saw and later, back at camp, email them to her. Oh, it didn't happen often, but he just couldn't—didn't—want to disappear out of her life. The flower photos kept them in touch with one another every few months and gave hope to his lonely heart, fed his tightly boxed and heavily protected emotions and lifted him, made him feel half-human, but the interactions also continued to stoke the flames of desire for her. Trudging slowly and reluctantly up the steps, he halted at the security door to the third floor, scowling, feeling like a coward. The envelope in his shirt pocket contained her orders. Ram had asked to deliver them personally to her and his boss gave his okay.

Recently, she was transferred to main HQ in Kyiv to continue her teaching duties. Sometimes, she would send him an email, but it would be of Adam Vorona's two young girls, Sofia and Anna, who were six and eight years old. She stayed with them at Adam's home in the village of Bucha, just outside of Kyiv, on weekends. Lera, his wife, would take photos of the three of them painting, drawing or looking at a bunch of plants and flowers spread out on the long wooden table in their kitchen.

He absorbed Dare's smile, the merriment in her eyes, as the girls would spontaneously wrap their small, thin arms around her waist or her neck, adoring her. They called her Auntie Dare. Those photos were

priceless to him: water on the desert of his heavily protected and unavailable heart. At times, he would pull
out his cell phone that the photos were on and absorb
them hungrily, starved for a little humanity. But in his
line of work? Emotions could get one killed. Worse,
the terror of one of his men getting killed because
he'd allowed his emotions to overwhelm his bear-trap
mental faculties that kept them all alive haunted him.

For whatever unknown reason, Dare sated his inner
emotional thirst, and it was that simple and that compli-
cated, not to mention a complete mystery to him. There
were no easy answers for Ram on the silent love he'd
carried for Dare over the years. He thought she was
still in Lviv, but he'd just found out the Ukraine Army
had transferred her to Kyiv six months ago.

His team had been on the move, sent over to the
United States for advanced training in certain weapons, and they'd just gotten back less than a week ago.
And now this: orders concerning Dare and his team.
They had this odd, out-of-kilter relationship, but there
was always a warm trust that simmered just below the
surface between them, never spoken about by either
of them. After all, he'd never let on how he really felt
about her. That was on him.

AFTER HER MORNING CLASS, Dare was finishing up packing the intubation mannequin used to teach her ten
Ukrainian medic students how to insert a tube into a
human throat. She hauled the bulky piece of luggage
to the closet at the back of the large room. The last
student from her class had departed ten minutes ear-

lier and she was almost finished with her duties before she left for the day. This was her classroom, with large windows showing the turbulent weather outside. Fondly, she looked around, loving her job, loving being in Ukraine. Since she spoke their language like a local, it was sheer enjoyment for her, as well.

Her students were surprised on the first day of class when she told them she had dual citizenship with the US and Ukraine. Her ability to speak their language was flawless, plus she knew a third language, Russian. She wore her US Army uniform, mottled gray, white and black camouflage fatigues, during the winter season.

Turning, she hauled the huge suitcase to the open closet, sliding it in, pushing it to the rear. There were many other medical cases piled high with apparatuses. Straightening, she was satisfied the case was where it needed to be.

There was a light knock at the door. Frowning, she backed out of the closet, looking toward it. Her lips parted. Her heart dropped and pounded in her chest as she stared right into the gold-brown eyes of Captain Ram Kozak. She moved from the closet, shutting it and then looking at where he stood in the partially opened door, his gaze as implacable and unreadable as usual.

She grinned. "Well, well, look what the cat dragged in," and she smiled fully, dusting off her hands as she walked toward him. A powerful warmth, much more than casual friendship, sizzled through her unexpectedly. Ram always made her feel feminine in the male world of the military. As CO and officer of his Black Wolf team, he had a powerful draw for her. Dare knew the military would never allow an officer and enlisted person, such as herself, to have a personal relationship with one another. It simply wouldn't happen. Swallowing her disappointment, she smiled in welcome as she drew near to him.

Ram entered the room. "You look well, Dare. Is everything going right in your world?"

She halted a few feet from him, speaking in Ukrainian. "Everything is fine," and then she grimaced. "Well, no, not everything. The Russians are coming," and she sighed. Pointing to a metal desk and chair, she said, "It's good to see you again. Come and sit down? I've been on my feet for three hours and my puppies are howling."

He managed a slight lift of one corner of his mouth, taking a seat at a desk that was opposite of where she sat, a few feet separating them. "You Americans have more strange sayings than I can keep track of, Dare."

She felt her face heating up. She was blushing just getting to sponge in Ram's always unreadable face. But his gold-colored eyes telling her he was happy to see her made her relax. "I know, we love our memes and sayings. How long has it been since we've last seen one another? Two years now since our last face-to-face?"

Nodding, he looked around the light, airy room. "I know you were teaching in Lviv, but I didn't know you had been transferred here to Kyiv six months ago.

Seems like so long ago. Does it to you?" He met and held her softening gaze.

"Sometimes it seems like yesterday and sometimes much longer than two years. I missed all of you," she admitted, losing her smile. "I talk to Adam often, and he fills me in on your team who just came back to Kyiv from many months of US training. He said they're awaiting a new assignment being given to you. Is that true?"

"We missed you, too. And yes, we've got a new assignment."

"I never know when you're around, Ram. Every time I tell Adam I should come over and see you, you're gone again. He'd told me you live in a village south of Kyiv."

"My apartment is an hour's drive from the city center. My team just spent twelve weeks in the US," he admitted. "While I was learning tactics and strategy at the Pentagon, the rest of my men went to a couple of other nearby Army bases. There was a group of field-grade officers who went on this training and education program, and I was selected to be one of them." He sighed. "With the Russians going to attack, the US Army offered to train us up on some things we were either rusty on or didn't know about, giving us the latest tactical advantages that they are sharing with us as a country. It was a useful time we spent in the States."

"Adam went with you," she said, nodding. "Lera, his wife, and I would spend weekends with the girls at their home in Bucha. She kept me updated on all of your travels to the US for special, ongoing training."

"Yes, some of my team were learning how to handle a Javelin tank killer that the US has. We received the intel and received the training we needed. It worked out well."

"I haven't spoken to Adam since he got home a few days ago. I'm sure he did well?"

"Yes. All my men passed their field tests. They are the best." He frowned and unbuttoned his shirt pocket, pulling out a folded piece of paper. "You know Adam—he's smart and catches on to new information fast. We have six men in our team who are now qualified to use the Javelin shoulder-carry weapon, and that's a relief to me. Our two snipers refined their skills at another base."

"Everyone thinks Putin will send tanks first into your country."

"In February of 2022. That's what our intel people say as well as what the Pentagon is confirming. Their intel people have been picking up a lot of unprotected cell phone chatter from the Russians," he admitted heavily. "They're coming in the dead of winter so that the soil is frozen and Putin's tanks can roll swiftly across the countryside to get into Ukraine and destroy us. If he tried to do that in January, the ground is still freezing."

"In March," Dare said, "it begins to thaw and his tanks will sink up to their drive sprocket in mud and the treads will come off and they'll be sitting ducks for those Javelins your guys have been trained on."

"Exactly right." He opened the paper and frowned.

"I've got some news that may be very upsetting to you, Dare."

She sat up, frowning. "Are those orders?"

"Yes."

"Don't tell me they're sending me back to the States, Ram. I won't go. My place is here. My adopted parents are Ukrainian. I feel this is my homeland, too, and I don't want to be sent away when the going gets tough around here."

He gave her a painful look and handed the paper to her. "I have no say in this. Read?"

She reached for the extended papers, her fingertips brushing his. The ache in her heart for this man, who was incredibly closed up, remained an enigma to her. How badly she wanted to know him on equal emotional footing, having been drawn to him since she met him in Afghanistan so long ago. The officer/enlisted issue always surfaced. She saw his eyes darken and he looked away for a moment, his mouth thinning and tightening.

The orders were written in Ukrainian and she could easily read them. Gasping, she managed in a strangled tone to say, "I'm being ordered back into *your team*? As your combat field medic?" She stared at the orders, reread them several times and then drilled a look into his unhappy looking gaze. "These are legit?" and she waved the papers in his direction. "Seriously, Ram? You're not playing a joke on me, are you?"

"I wish it was a joke," he answered heavily, pushing his fingers through his short, dark hair after taking off his cap. "It's for real, Dare."

"Wow," she uttered, amazed and shocked. "I'm on your team again?"

"Yes. My CO wanted to call you in, but I asked if I could break the news to you myself."

Setting the paper aside on the desk, she muttered, "You don't sound happy about this, Ram. Are *you* okay with this?"

He sat up, pushing his large hands palm down on the thighs of his winter fatigues, holding her gaze. "On a personal level? This is the last place I'd want you to be, Dare. On a professional level, you are fully competent in the field. Everyone knows you are reliable and a strong team member. Everyone trusts you. We wouldn't be breaking in a new field medic, so for the team? I know they'll be happy to have you returning to our fold."

Scowling, she reread the orders. "Did you ask for me?" she demanded, holding his narrowing gaze.

"Hell no! I want you safe. I wanted you out of our country. What's coming early sometime next year are Russians who never take prisoners. You've never seen them in action, and I have." He snapped his mouth shut, a lot of emotions boiling to the surface within him, coloring his tone of voice. He shook his head, giving her an apologetic look for his sudden outburst.

Dare blinked in shock over his unexpected outburst. It was completely out of character for him to become so emotional. It set her spinning and she didn't have time to analyze why. There was anguish in his face for a split second and then it was gone. Feeling like she'd been wrapped in a sudden, violent storm, she dragged in a deep breath, the silence hanging jaggedly between them. "The men and women in my class have been talking about the Russian invasion. I've heard all the war stories, Ram. I understand how brutal they are."

His fist had clenched on the desk and he forced himself to try to relax. "I know firsthand what they are capable of, Dare. I don't want you out in the field with anyone, not even my team. It's not safe…"

Her mouth quirked and she laid the orders aside. "War is never safe and we both know that," she parried gently. "The Taliban and ISIS were just as evil and brutal as the Russians."

He shook his head, his voice dropping to a growl. "No… I can make that comparison, and you can't. I've seen firsthand what they are capable of doing and I don't want you out in the field at all, with anyone, not even my team."

"I suppose you told your CO that?" She saw a tortured expression in his gaze for a fleeting moment before that poker face of his moved back into place.

"I told my CO that I didn't want you in the field." He swallowed hard, looked away and then held her steady gaze. "I lost the argument with him because he knows your service record and courage. I pleaded with him to let you stay on as an instructor-educator, not to be sent out onto the battlefield." His voice lowered and he shook his head. "Our two years in Afghanistan with you as a member made him adamant that you were going back into the field with us because the higher-ups were desperate for your skills and experience."

"Because we were a good team and got the job done. I know our stats for locating and finding the enemy were consistently high. But it wasn't just me. It was the whole team working as one."

Unhappily he stared at her. "Yes, we were too damned good together, the ten of us. You saved Artur's life, and my CO was very impressed with the field surgery you performed on him. I couldn't argue against that. In the end? He gave me a choice. Either take you on as our field combat medic or find another one to replace you and he'd then assign you to another SSO team." Wearily, he rasped, "Either way, Dare, you were going back out into the battlefield and I told him I wanted you with our team. That I didn't want you assigned to someone else."

She sighed. "Ram, Ukraine is my country, too, my people."

He frowned. "I always wondered why a US Army medic was assigned to Ukraine and to our team."

"You never asked." She grinned a little, seeing humor for a moment skitter across his gaze. "You're a man of few words, Ram. And you weren't exactly personal with any of us."

"Yeah, I know I'm not touchy-feely."

She managed a slight laugh. "Oh, I don't think anyone on your team would *ever* accuse you of being that." And then she gave him a teasing look. "Do you know what I started calling you when we were over in Afghanistan?"

He straightened, scowling. "What?"

"In my head, I called you a teddy bear. You were all grizzly bear outside, but inside, you had a heart, you cared for and loved everyone on your team, you were super protective of them and you were ruthless with yourself when it came to planning an op and having it go off right, not wrong."

His mouth twisted. "Well, you're right about that. I'm the team leader. It's my responsibility to keep you all alive."

"I saw the teddy bear side of you when Artur was badly wounded," she ventured softly. "Up until that time, Ram? I wondered if you had a heart at all…"

Wincing, he avoided her saddened look. "That's *your* job, Dare, not mine. There is no room on the field of battle for emotions and you know that."

His snapping at her made her sit up a little more. She saw the hurt in his eyes fleetingly when she'd accused him of not having a heart. "I'm sorry," she offered quietly, holding his stare. "I shouldn't have said that. It was wrong. Everyone has a heart." She opened her hands. "It's just that—" she searched for the right words "—you're so unreadable to me…to us…the team. There have been times when all of us have cried out on an op, and that was when Artur was wounded. I cried through my tears as I stitched him up and I prayed to God that he could save him because I wasn't sure he would live. Artur was one of our most favorite guys who always wore his heart on his sleeve…"

Gruffly, he said, "Artur and Adam are like that. Maybe I should pay attention to the fact that both have names that start with an A. Those two were the class clowns on the team, sometimes."

She smiled a little. "They were our comic relief, Ram. They helped all of us climb down off that dangerous cliff we always tread. They helped us laugh when we got back to camp, all in one piece, no one killed. They reminded me of a TV show called *Saturday Night Live*, where fun was poked at politicians and other events and even though they were real and sometimes awful, you watched and you laughed because they found something funny about it. Those two were truly our relief valves. Artur and Adam acted out for all of us, and it was healing."

Ram stared at her. "Yes...they did... I still miss Artur. Although he is now out of the Army, he is alive, his wife and children are happy he is home with them, and he's learning a whole new trade now, creating wood sculptures. Did you know that?"

"Yes, I did. Artur's injuries were too severe for him to ever stay in the military after that wounding, but he's found an outlet for himself and his wood sculptures, according to Adam, and they are now sold to high-end retail stores. He makes a good living for himself and his family. I'm so happy for him. And relieved..."

"I'll never forget when he was wounded," Ram admitted heavily. "We were under constant fire and you risked your life to drag him to safety while we initiated cover fire for both of you. I was so afraid you'd die out there, too..."

She blinked and absorbed his unexpected emotional

admittance. And just as quickly, that angst in his expression disappeared. Had she really seen and heard him being emotional? This wasn't the time or place to pursue it, either. "Well," she whispered, "I was scared as hell as I ran out there to drag him to safety. I wasn't sure I'd live to see the next second, but I wasn't going to let him lay out there and bleed to death, either."

"I remember screaming at you not to go," he grunted. "You didn't listen."

She chuckled. "Surely you know a combat medic takes the job without the frills, Ram. It was *my job* to go after Artur. He was exposed. I was to protect and save him. I was the right person for that moment."

He slid her a glance. "I remember it all… That was such a hot mess of an op. Everything that could go wrong did go wrong."

"Except it was Sergeant Kuzma Pavlenko, our comms, who managed to get a US Army Chinook helicopter diverted and to come and get Artur to the base for an emergency operation to save his life. That was something that went right."

"Kuz saved the day," Ram agreed quietly, folding his hands between opened thighs. "Without him…"

"My field surgery made it possible for him to survive for that 'golden hour,'" she admitted, "but without Kuz finding and locating that nearby Chinook, which was already on one mission, diverting instead to help Artur…" She shook her head. "I'm good at what I do, Ram, but I fully admit that without Kuz persuading the pilots to turn and come and help us, I'm positive

Artur would not have made it. He had one hour, and that was it."

There was a mixture of emotions in his expression again. Had he changed over the last two years? Was he softening up, as she called it, and showing how he felt? That was good in her estimation. No one liked talking to the ice castle that he'd been with the team when she was on board with them. Dare fully realized every one of them, regardless of gender, had to handle a helluva lot of emotions that could not get in the way when they were out on an op. For her, the trick was how to climb down off that mental cliff afterward.

Like everyone else on the team, at camp, she would sometimes wake up screaming, or a flashback would occur and she'd shout or scream, waking herself up, as well as her teammates who slept in the same plywood building. She wasn't the only one. Every man, with the exception of Ram Kozak, did the same thing. Getting a full night's sleep behind the wire was not guaranteed at all. It was just part of their job. The emotions suppressed during an op came surging up as they slept in the guise of a dream or, worse, a nightmare.

Ram sat up, moving his shoulders to shed the tension out of them. "We were a good team, Dare. That is what stopped Artur from dying."

Nodding, she said, "He's got a decent life now. Adam told me he makes good money for his family off his creativity. Who knew he was such a skilled, artistic sculptor?"

Shaking his head, Ram muttered, "I often wonder

who or what I'd have been if my life had turned out differently. Don't you?" He met her serious-looking gaze.

"Oh," she said, rolling her eyes, "don't go there, Ram. My life is more like a patchwork quilt thrown together. If you'd have asked me if I thought my career would be in the military and I'd be a combat medic? In my early teens, I'd have laughed and said that you were wrong." Her grin widened and she opened her arms. "But look at me now. This is who I am. As a child I never dreamed this dream."

He sat back, thoughtful. "You realize we've *never* talked like this with one another before?"

"What do you mean?"

"I mean," and he searched for the right word, "*personally*?"

"From the moment I was assigned to your team in Afghanistan, you instilled in me that it was your way or the highway. Remember? No touchy-feely? No crying? No getting depressed? No having a bad day? We were all supposed to be like automatons, heartless, using only strong mental focus and that was it so the job got accomplished and the team came back in one piece. Oh, I remember those times, all right."

"You're here," he deadpanned, "alive and in one piece. The whole team came home. You can't argue with success, Dare."

A bit of laughter rolled out of her. "Well, I think Artur nearly dying broke everyone."

"It did," he admitted, rubbing his stubbled jaw. "I've changed a little," he admitted wryly. "Artur reminded me of my younger brother, Alex, and I always appreciated his sense of humor, his comedy of errors he always pretended to make in order to give the team a laugh…"

Tilting her head, she studied him in the silence. "I didn't know you had a brother. His name was Alex?" Instantly she saw that hard, expressionless mask drop over his face. Ram became stiff and his gold eyes turned thundercloud dark. Tension flowed through her as she saw him wrestling with some invisible and yet obviously very painful memory to him. She didn't have the courage to ask more, seeing his swift reaction.

Ram jabbed his finger at the orders lying on the desk before her. "Do you really want to go out in the battlefield with us?"

Distraction. Okay, she could understand it. "Of course I do. We're a known quantity to one another. I would think you'd be overjoyed to have nine of the ten original members back together for this coming war."

He nodded. "Sergeant Symon Kravets, who everyone calls Zap, has replaced Artur. He's a satellite and computer expert for our team now. I think you'll like him. He's sharp, fast and obsessed with anything electronic."

She saw him beginning to relax once more…well, as much as Ram *could* relax. To her he was always like an explosive that at any time could blow up. He never had when they were together, but the feeling was still there. Wondering if his family was a sore topic for whatever reason, she realized that sense of tightly controlled emotions was back and it was almost palpable to her. Dare blamed her super sensitivity, her intuition and ability to feel things most men ignored. There had been several times in Afghanistan when she'd sensed danger, where it was located and it had always panned out. In her second year of being with the team, it got so that they relied heavily upon what they called her: the psychic in the group. Dare took it with gracefulness, laughed it off, but still, even Ram listened to her when she picked up or sensed danger nearby. Adam had teased her that she was actually a killer K-9 Belgian Malinois incarnated into a human body in order to save the team's "collective ass," as he called it. Everyone got a huge laugh out of that one. Even Ram, who barely cracked one, grinned over that joke.

"Zap," she laughed softly, "what a great nickname for the new member of the team!"

"You'll like him," Ram said, relaxing a little. "He's young, a twenty-year-old, starry-eyed about being in a black ops unit and all. Said he grew up as a user of combat software games."

"He hasn't been in combat yet to know the difference…"

"No, but he will find out."

"Good thing the rest of team is blooded," she said quietly. "It will help him adjust when the time comes. They'll be support for him as he goes through his own personal shock and trauma. I'm sure he'll realize real war is nothing like his software games."

"Yeah," he muttered, sitting up. "Part of the initiation for becoming black ops. Kill or be killed. It's black or white."

"Is someone taking him under their wing?"

"Kuz is doing it," Ram said. "He's a father by nature, you know that."

She smiled a little. "Well, after all, he has three darling children and a wonderful wife. I'd say he has a lot of good father attributes he can shower on Zap." Most of the men were married, or at least when she left the team in Afghanistan they were. Every once in a while, she'd hear about one of them, usually via voluble comic, Adam, or his wife, Lera, about a team member's personal life, a new baby coming along to be celebrated or someone getting married.

"Kuz has an interest in the computer side of comms, and that's what drew them together. But it's a good thing because Zap is pretty immature." He made a motion with his fingers toward his head. "The kid is green and has all these naive ideas about gaming black ops. I don't think that under ordinary circumstances they'd let someone of his age and idealism into a team like ours, but we're going to need his expertise out in the field like never before. And this is a different war that's going to be waged versus the one we went through in Afghanistan. The Russians will be throwing their best computer hackers at our software programs, trying to mess them up or delete or freeze them so we can't use them."

"I see," she murmured. "Do you feel he'll be a fit?"

Shrugging, Ram said, "That remains to be seen, but I've talked to Kuz privately about my concerns regarding the kid, and he's in agreement with me. Kuz will keep his ass close to his own. And when we enter combat, Zap will have someone who can protect, guide and teach him on the fly. It's as good as it's going to get. Black ops is bloody and murderous, nothing short of that, and Zap has this starry-eyed combat software gamer's idea in his head of what it will be like."

"It's nothing like that," she agreed, sadness in her tone. Once more, she was seeing Ram being more emotional than usual. Clearly, he was worried about Zap being initiated into a live-fire situation where life, death or being taken prisoner was on the line. The kid had nothing to compare real life with the canned software gamer life he'd led before.

"I'm sure you can help him, too," Ram added, giving her a hopeful look. "You were always 'mother' to all of us on the team."

Snorting, Dare grinned wickedly. "You warned me right off the bat not to mother the guys. What's this? All of a sudden looking for a mommy in the group now?"

He had the good grace to manage a twist of his mouth. "You're right, of course. I didn't want you mothering my men."

"And it didn't happen. But obviously, that's a secret fear you held about me? That I'd do that?"

"I guess I was hoping you might let some of that mommy side of you show to Zap. I think the kid is going to need a 'dad' and a 'mom' for a while as he gets rid of his gamer reality and trades it in for the hard-core reality of what war is really like, instead. It's going to throw him and I can't have the kid losing it and forgetting what he's supposed to be doing out in the field working with us."

"It's a delicate balance," Dare agreed, frowning. "I'll do what I can."

He looked at the watch on his wrist. "I must go. Did Adam invite you over to his home in Bucha, yet?"

"Yes, he called me last night. I usually spend weekends with him, Lera and the kids. I act as kind of a babysitter and housekeeper for them."

"And what does that give you?" Ram wondered.

"I get to practice my mothering skills."

He laughed sourly and shook his head, standing. "Touché, you nailed me."

"You're an easy target, Captain."

He placed the hat on his head, lowering the bill. "Well, I sure walked into that one with you, but no one said you were asleep at the switch, either."

"Never will be." She stood, folding the orders and placing them in a ziplock pocket on the left thigh of her fatigues. "When I talked to Adam yesterday he said there was a secret visitor coming for the weekend to stay with them. Is that you?"

"You're good, Dare. Really good. You must have that psychic switch turned on right now."

Grinning wolfishly, she walked up to the desk and retrieved her knapsack, pulling it over her shoulders. "Well, I didn't know until just now. It makes sense that Adam knew because he's second-in-command,

and I would be there babysitting this weekend and he wanted to get you out of that combat environment and let you ramp down for a weekend."

"I told him I'd stay tonight and leave on Sunday afternoon."

"Good. You need to be around people who love you."

Chapter Two

November 1

By the time Dare got off the bus at her fourteen-story apartment building near the center of Kyiv, her thoughts remained centered on Ram. It was 1300, 1:00 p.m. She had time to change, get a shower, pack a small suitcase and drive out to Bucha, the village where Adam and Lera lived. She liked spending her weekends with them whenever possible.

Ram...the enigma. She'd walked out of his life two years ago and it had been heart-wrenching for her because she'd secretly fallen in love with the hardened warrior who let no one into his inner life. He was all business. Always. Why?

After slipping the code card into the slot of her ground-floor apartment, she pushed the door open with her boot and it closed automatically behind her. Even though it was a rainy, gray day, the three massive floor-to-ceiling windows made her two-bedroom apartment look bright. After placing her briefcase and several other items into the guest bedroom, she went across the hall to climb out of her military gear and slip into a quick, hot shower. That always revived and centered her. She slowly inhaled the rose-scented soap, its delicious fragrance filling her lungs. So, she was going to war—again. The shock still reverberated within her.

Dare was older now, twenty-nine, not a young twenty-five-year-old when she'd been ordered to Ram's black ops unit in Afghanistan. It had been an adventure to her, a challenge she readily accepted, but she soon found out that learning combat medicine in a schoolroom didn't even come close to being out in the field where life and death was a breath away from every member of the team. After two years, she was ready to leave the war-torn fields of Afghanistan, overjoyed at the Lviv, Ukraine, assignment to teach field combat medicine to the medics of this wonderful country.

Ram...

She scrubbed her hair and rinsed beneath the streams of water, trying to tame her powerful feelings of joy intertwined with the shock of him walking back into her life once again.

What was she going to do? What should she do? Was it really orders from higher up that assigned her back to his team? Or did he have something to do with it? Her gut told her someone above him in rank had made that decision because he didn't seem particularly happy to see her back with his unit. Worse, as she stepped out of the shower, grabbing a pale yellow bath towel, starting to dry herself off, she'd seen and felt conflicting emotions around him. Did he not want her on his team again? There had been a cross-current within him, but she couldn't suss it out any more than that. Being a sensitive, somewhat psychic individual, she hated that she'd gotten a hit on it but not the whole story. And usually, that made her impatient and frustrated. Ram Kozak was not the kind of man to let her see what cards he held in his hand and he wasn't about to show them to her now, either.

She hated him being like a Rubik's Cube and she could never figure him out or sense the feelings around him that he'd never given voice to. Yet, as she sat down on the chair and put on a pair of warm, lambswool socks, then pulled on her loose-fitting jeans and a lambswool, long-sleeved pink sweater, she never knew how he really felt or thought. Even Adam, who was close to Ram, like a brother, didn't know his backstory. Where was he born? Where was his family? Where did they live? He never talked about them, and family was everything to the Ukrainian people, so tightly knit and woven together. Adam's parents were dead now, and he lived in the same village and in the same house he'd been born in. She loved that about Ukraine. In the USA, it was vastly different. Extended family didn't necessarily live in the same house or even town.

After combing her short crop of black hair, using her fingers to fluff it up a bit, she tidied up the bathroom, left the door open and headed for the kitchen.

Ram...

As she made herself some coffee, hips resting against the counter, arms across her breasts, she stared down at the colorful tile floor. How shocked, curious and stunned she still felt by today's unexpected event.

She realized Ram had changed from her Afghanistan days with him. He was, well, almost warm toward her, showing a little emotion here and there, which had been completely MIA, missing in action, before. He even cracked a partial smile earlier, which truly stunned her. Their conversation was far more personal, a giving and taking, than it ever had been before. Had he changed because of some incident she didn't know about? He was older now. Or was this the "real" Ram, a man who had a rich tapestry of emotions just like any other human being possessed and was allowing them some airtime? Behind his back, she always thought of him as Ram the Robot. A robot didn't have a heart and possessed no emotions. Just a head full of mental activity and focus was all. This latest version of Ram was far nicer, a tad more open, even a hint of emotion in his gruff voice now and then. All new!

What had changed him, she wondered. Maybe Adam could shed some light on it since he'd been with the team those two years after she'd left. Two years was a long time, she conceded. A lot could have happened. Adam would be the one to talk with and he'd give her the intel. Maybe then she could figure out this new 2.0 version of Ram and understand it and him better. She had to, because she was going out in the field with him again.

The coffee was ready. She put a dab of honey and cream into the mug and went to the living room, sitting down in her rocking chair. Moving it slowly back and forth, the coffee between her hands, she frowned. *Combat. Once again.* She had PTSD, but anyone in black ops got that as entrance to the dark games they played behind the scenes with their enemies. Everyone was on war footing in Ukraine and she could see the worry and strain in everyone's face. They knew what was coming, but she also knew the lion strength of the people's heart to live in a democracy, too. She knew it would rip Ukraine up, but the people were stalwart and fighters. Putin didn't know what he was biting off by trying to steal their land and break their will, trying to make everyone Russian by proxy. That would *never* happen.

Looking up at the ceiling, she sighed. She knew her adopted parents, who lived in Cleveland, Ohio, were worried about it, too. They held dual citizenship, like she did. They had adopted her at three months old after she was left on the steps of an Ohio fire department station. She had no memory of it. Her adopted mother, Maria, and father, Panas Mazur, a world-renowned cardiologist surgeon, had loved her from the moment she was brought to them. They had lived outside the city, in a rural area with a big farmhouse, barn and fifty acres of land. They flew back once a year, to their home, Lviv, Ukraine, near the Polish border, and saw their large, extended family. She had grown up visiting her Ukrainian relatives and always looked forward to seeing them. Half her soul was a part of their beautiful country, and the other half was where she was born in the USA. A foot in two worlds.

Dare preferred the warm, huge, tight Ukrainian family lifestyle. Her parents would stay a month in Lviv and she loved the huge celebratory family gatherings, the women bringing all their favorite dishes, the home smelling of rosemary, basil, garlic and so many other wonderful herbal scents. The Ukrainian people had beautiful ceremonies and dances and she loved the bright costumes, the energy and heart in their songs and movements.

She'd been overjoyed when the US Army had given her a two-year teaching position in Lviv to train Ukrainian Army medics to be even more important in combat than before.

Her mind turned to Adam and Lera, and their two spunky little daughters, Anna and Sofia. She was so at home with them and even though she had her own apartment in Kyiv, she routinely spent weekends with them, starting on Friday night and driving out to their village, one of the two spare bedrooms hers, the children anxiously awaiting her arrival. Her weekends were so much fun, filled with laughter, giggling and exciting exploration outdoors with the children. Their two red-haired daughters followed her around like happy, wriggling puppies in search of a new adventure. Dare loved exploring with them, the woods nearby offering so much to learn about and such wonderful edible wild mushrooms that one could eat with their evening meals. She was teaching the girls how to identify the edibles from the poisonous ones. Lera had begun to teach them, and show them how to always cook them first, and use them in casseroles, soups and stews. Yes, she eagerly looked forward to spending time with them. Dare considered them her second family, feeling very lucky and enriched by her caring Ukrainian friends.

Finishing off her coffee, she looked over at the top of her TV. There were lots of framed photos, some of her mother and father, Adam's entire family. Her gaze drifted to the last one: Ram Kozak. Dare stared at the warrior, his face set, three-day growth of beard, in black ops gear, staring flatly back at her. She smiled a little, remembering that time. He hated pictures of himself, but she'd caught him off guard one day, lying in wait for him because she knew his habits and routine at the camp, and got the photo. He wasn't very happy about it, but she'd seen a bit of pluckiness about him after she told him she really wanted a photo of him for her family album.

Ram was still a part of her. Much larger than she wanted to admit. Now? Everything had changed in a snap of the cosmic fingers of Fate. They were together again. A unit. A family...

November 2

"COME IN!" Lera sang, wiping her hands on her apron, smiling at Dare, who had her arms filled with two large paper grocery sacks.

"I'm a little late," she said, breathless, hurrying inside their large village home. It was warm compared with outside, the wind cutting and cold.

"You're never late!" Lera said, taking one of the

sacks. "You didn't have to do this, Dare, you know that!" She hurried over to the long kitchen counter with one of the bulging sacks. The area was huge, with a long trestle table with twelve chairs around it. Outside the large bank of windows, the trees were bending with the gusts of rain and wind from the cold front coming through.

"Are we going to have Ram over for dinner?" Dare asked, setting the second sack down on the kitchen counter, unloading all the items to be put into the fridge or the cabinets. She saw Lera's green eyes twinkle. She had her red hair, which was long and could go halfway down her back, twisted into two red braids and then wound up on top of her head. She too wore jeans and a comfy orange sweater that showed off her shining auburn hair.

"Yes! First time ever. Adam had invited him to have dinner and stay overnight with us, but he always turned us down." She grinned. "I think he's invited himself over here because *you* are here."

Snorting, taking the sour cream and other containers across the room to the fridge, Dare said, "I had no idea he was coming until he told me himself earlier today."

"You saw him?" Her eyes went wide with surprise.

Once she placed the items in the fridge, she shut the door and turned. "Yes. Didn't he tell Adam that orders were cut for me to rejoin his team?"

Gasping, her hands flew to her mouth. Lera stared in shock at her. "No! When did this happen?"

Dare patted her small shoulder. Lera was only five

feet six inches tall, slender, but a human dynamo who was always in motion. Dare blamed it on her red hair. "It's okay, Lera. I was in shock just seeing him. It has been two years since I've seen him in person. I didn't even know he was in Kyiv. That was six months ago. In the last email I received from him, he said his team was in the US learning new things. And that they just returned a few days ago."

"Adam returned last week ahead of the team," Lera said pertly, quickly disgorging the rest of the contents from the sack to the counter. "You did not know Ram was here in Kyiv, then?"

"Not at all."

"Well, the whole team has been in the USA with the Army training programs on different kinds of weapons," Lera said. "Adam never talked much about it because, as you know, everything in an SSO team is top-secret."

"Sure is," Dare agreed, reaching up to put a box of cornmeal onto a shelf that was hard for Lera to reach without her constant companion, a nearby oak stool.

"Still," Lera persisted, frowning as she folded the sacks and put them away, "Ram has never been over to our home, never asked to come over and share a meal with us. He's always been standoffish and politely turned down Adam's invites to be with us every time."

Dare was familiar with the kitchen and Lera's needs as the chief cook, and she would assist her. "Have you seen Ram at all?"

"No," Lera said. "Why?"

"Well," she murmured, "he's changed somewhat since I last saw him in Afghanistan."

"Oh?" Her red brows arched, interest in her eyes. "How do you mean that?"

"Usually he's like a blank whiteboard. You can't read him at all. I never could tell when I was on his team if he was happy, sad, depressed or whatever about me. This time, when he saw me after my class was over at the institute, he was…" She hesitated, searching for the right word. "Well… He wasn't a whiteboard this time."

Lera walked over to a large glass baking dish where she was fixing a meal for all of them tonight. "You've always said he couldn't be read. Adam says the same thing. He is a very closet-like person, Dare. That hasn't changed, or has it?"

Dare brought over a kitchen knife and saw the cucumbers that needed to be sliced and diced and put in the half-made potato salad. "Don't know. He just… well…seemed more open, but I wouldn't get excited about it. Maybe a crack, not opening the door so you could see what he was feeling and conveying it. Just a hint here and there. That's what changed. And I don't know if that was a one-time thing with him or if he's actually opening up a bit to the rest of the world."

Lera placed the finishing touches on a large pan of chicken Kyiv, a country favorite. The chicken filets had been well pounded, rolled around in butter mixed with fresh dill, and then coated with a mixture of egg and dried bread crumbs. She lifted up the large baking dish and Dare followed, opening the oven door for her. "Thank you," Lera said, grinning and shutting the door. "So? His behavior is finally thawing, perhaps?"

Chuckling, Dare went back to her workstation, finishing off the diced cucumbers and starting on the hard-boiled eggs and dicing them. "*Thaw* is a good word that I was searching for," she told Lera. The woman had a pleased, foxy look in her expression. "What's that look for?" Dare demanded.

"Ohhh, my," Lera trilled, pulling out some cooling garlic bread she'd made. *Pampushky* was wonderful and one of Dare's favorites. It was a dinner bread with a sweet taste, the texture billowy, and the garlic, butter and parsley brushed on it after it had browned filled the air with the mouthwatering scents. "Don't you think it kismet that here you are in town and he's coming back from the USA and has Adam invite him to dinner? Hmm?" She arched one eyebrow, her grin turning positively merry.

Dare knew that feral look. "Don't go there," she warned, slicing the vegetable. "I think he was worried how I'd react to being taken out of the classroom teaching and then summarily dropped back into his team."

Brushing the garlic bread with swift, knowing strokes, it was Lera's turn to snort. "There's more to this! Does he know you are still single and free? No attachments?"

"We didn't discuss anything that personal," Dare said. "Not that he ever showed an interest in who may or may not be in my life."

"You know that he's still not attached?" Lera said, her smile widening. "Neither of you are. He's thirty years old and you're twenty-nine. You should both be married by now, Dare."

It was Dare's turn to snort. She picked up a large spoon to turn over the potato salad and mix it. "Just haven't met the right person, I guess," she answered a bit defensively.

"You know what I really think?" Lera said, coming over and patting her shoulder.

"You've never held back before and you're on a roll. Why stop now?"

Cackling, Lera gripped her shoulder gently and whispered, "I think he's wanted a relationship with you for a long, long time because that would explain why he's still unattached and why he's invited himself to dinner tonight. And," she shook her finger at Dare, "he's staying over the whole weekend. Did you know *that*?"

Blinking owlishly, Dare stared down at the triumphant, know-it-all look on Lera's thin face that was sprinkled with freckles. She groaned. The spoon in her hand stopped midair. "He did mention he'd be coming to dinner and staying over until Sunday morning. But I honestly do not think it's because I'm here."

"Then, you tell me your idea of why he's invited himself for this weekend. Adam invited him to Friday night dinner. He did not invite him to stay the whole weekend. Now, how did that happen? And why? We do have two guest bedrooms, that's not a problem. I'm sure Adam told him you would be coming over Friday night through Sunday afternoon, living with us for a bit, and perhaps that is why he's coming. *You* will be here!"

She gave Lera a rolled-eye look, forcing herself to pay attention to stirring up the potato salad. "I think you've gone bonkers."

"What does *bonkers* mean?" Lera demanded, her hands now on her hips. "Your American slang drives me to distraction."

"Wild."

Laughing sharply, she shook her head and took the garlic bread, placing it in the warmer above the stove after covering it with a towel. "It's the only good explanation as to why he'll be here shortly. He and Adam are driving back and will be here around five for dinner."

"Occam's razor," Dare muttered sourly, shaking her head.

"You're muttering again. You only do that when you are upset. Who is Occam?"

"He was a fourteenth-century logician and theologian. His name was William of Ockham. His theory states 'the simplest solution is almost always best.'"

Snickering, Lera said triumphantly, "I was right! Mr. Occam agrees with *me*!"

Dare shook her head, giving her a teasing look. "We'll see," she said, "we'll see… Don't forget, he's an officer, and I'm an enlisted person, Lera. We could never have any kind of personal relationship, anyway. The military would not allow it."

"You have always confided in me," Lera reminded her. "You admitted that you were very drawn to Ram, enlisted or otherwise. Yes? Eh?"

"I was… Well, I still am, and that's bonkers, too. The only time I heard from him was an email every couple of months with a photograph of a flower he took while on a mission. He knows I love flowers. I can't read any more into it than that."

Lera couldn't help but allow herself to smile fully. "And why would any man take that kind of time to do something like that for two years after you have been separated? Eh?" Lera poked her finger into Dare's upper arm. "How did it make you feel when he sent you those photos?"

Sighing, Dare put a lid over the potato salad and walked it to the refrigerator. "It always made me happy, Lera."

"Seriously," she opined. "You know? You two remind me of the old Victorian era where a man would court a woman he loved sometimes for years before he would ask for her hand in marriage. No kissing. No touching. No honesty about how each other really felt toward one other…" She snorted and shook her head, throwing her hands up in frustration.

Dare grinned a little. "You're such a firecracker, Lera." She gently hugged the small woman. Releasing her, she said, "It's that red hair of yours on fire again. Okay, in my deepest, dark parts of myself, I felt he cared for me enough to send those flower photos. He knows how much I love botany."

"This is going to become very interesting," Lera said, taking a washcloth and wiping down the counter with quick, knowing strokes.

"Don't you and Adam stare at us over dinner, Lera.

We aren't bugs under a collective microscope to be watched for some change in our nonrelationship."

"Oh," she laughed, "we wouldn't do that! What will be interesting," and she looked at her watch, "is how the girls will react to Ram. They've never met him."

"Now, that's something I can agree with you on," Dare laughed.

"You do like him still, don't you?"

"Yes," she admitted quietly.

"And it's serious. Yes?"

She gave Lera disheartened look. "Yes, but it's not going anywhere. If he was really serious about me— and he never showed one iota that he was—don't you think he'd have come clean, been honest with me, if that was so?"

"He's a strange one, I will give you that." Lera slid her arm around Dare's waist. "He's not like everyone else, from what Adam has shared with me. I've never met him, either, so I'm very interested in his reactions to me and the girls, and to you, of course."

It was 4:00 p.m., and Dare saw Adam drive in with the girls in his car. "He's got the kids," she called to Lera.

"Good. Now, we're one happy family again. Ram will be arriving an hour from now!"

RAM HATED LIKE hell to admit it, but he was nervous. That was one emotion that he thought had been crushed and destroyed a long time ago. As he parked his car in the driveway of Adam's home at 5:00 p.m., the sky was darkening with more rain to come. Turning off the engine, he stared at the passenger seat. There was a two-pound box of chocolates for Lera. He'd never met Adam's wife before, and he wanted to make a good impression with her. Adam talked a lot about his fiery red-haired wife and Ram thought he knew enough about her. What put him on edge was Dare. She would be there already, seeing another car in the driveway. He stared over at the mixed bouquet of fresh flowers for her. He knew she would like them.

He sat there for a moment, feeling the terrible past clawing at him. He'd slammed a door so damned tightly on it that he thought it would never visit him again. For whatever twisted, dark reason, the last two years without Dare being with him, he would dream of having a family. And she was his wife. He'd always wake up, of course, breathing hard, sweating, shaking and wanting to sob for the losses he'd suffered. He would sit up in bed, and look around the darkened apartment bedroom, wondering why these silly dreams were happening. Why now?

He would never put anyone through what he experienced. No one. Especially Dare. He cared too much for her. His desire to make her his was sometimes nearly overwhelming. He'd never touched her. Never kissed her. Never spoke of his real feelings he had for her. No, he'd kept a very tight rein on them when she joined their team and lived with them in their plywood quarters at the top-secret camp in Afghanistan.

Trying to put a lid on his past, he looked at the two brightly wrapped gifts next to the flowers and chocolates. These presents were for their two young daughters. He wanted to make a good impression with all of them and he didn't question himself too deeply as to why. Since eighteen, he'd lived his life like a monk in a cave. He wanted no emotional strings attached to anyone at any time except for the safety of his team and trying to keep them alive to go home to their families.

He girded himself internally, placed the gifts and box into a sack and held the bouquet as he climbed out of his car. The wind was gusty and the temperature was dropping. As he closed the door, he wondered if there would be rain or snow to follow. That would be early in the season and the thought nagged him because if the ground grew hard and frozen earlier than usual, it meant the Russians would attack them sooner with their tank columns that were amassing right now near the Ukraine border. Pulling the sheepskin collar of his aviation leather jacket around his neck, he hurried up to the front door.

He barely got the doorbell rung when the door flew open. There were two little redheaded girls, both dressed in jeans and warm, long-sleeved sweaters, their hair in pigtails, waving their arms and smiling up at him, while simultaneously jumping up and down for joy. Adam squeezed between his daughters and pushed the screen door open for him.

"Come on in, Ram. Girls…girls," he pleaded, "let Ram get in the door before you attack him."

Ram smiled a little, shook his head and moved into the warm house filled with many wonderful fragrances of food cooking in the kitchen. It brought back so many happy memories of his family to him.

Adam shut the door, grinning. "They've been very curious who my boss was, and when I told them you were going to have dinner with us? They've been watching for you to drive in so they could greet you first."

"Well," Ram said, eyeing both girls, who now had settled down, their hands clasped in front of them, looking shyly up at him, "that is very nice." He set the sack down, crouched down on the hardwood floor and pulled out two gifts from it. He gave one to each of them. "For you," he said, watching their surprise as they took them.

"You didn't have to do that," Adam said.

Ram straightened. "Best to get off on the right foot?" He saw his second-in-command nod and give him a silly, knowing grin.

"Come on, girls, show Ram to the kitchen, where we'll be eating."

Ram followed as the girls galloped ahead like young wild horses. A pain hit his heart, an old memory from the past striking him squarely in the chest. He'd lost two of his cousins, both young girls about their age, at eighteen. Never to see them grow up. Never to see them fall in love, get married and be happy. Pushing the memories back, he followed Adam into the large, pale yellow kitchen that filled his nostrils with so many good flavors that his mouth watered. It all reminded him of his mother's, grandmother's and aunt's cooking, and again that old grief-stricken pain struck his heart.

"Lera?" Adam called. "Come meet my boss, Captain Ram Kozak…"

Lera smiled and placed the chicken Kyiv on the table. Wiping her hands on her apron, she came over and shook his hand. "We're glad to finally meet you, Captain. You're more than welcome at our home. You're a part of our larger family now."

Ram nodded and shook her thin, small hand. "I brought you something," he said and dug into the sack, producing the chocolates. "Call me Ram? These are for you. Everything you're making smells wonderful. Thank you for all the time it took for you to make it for all of us."

Smiling, Lera said, "You've very kind and thoughtful, Ram. I can see my daughters are eyeballing my box of chocolates already. I think I'm going to have to hide it from them."

Adam laughed and took the box, placing it high on a cabinet where the girls would never be able to reach. They loved chocolate like their mother did.

Ram looked around. "I thought Dare was here? That she was going to have dinner with us?"

"She'll be here in a minute," Lera said. "Those flowers are for her?"

"Yes."

Lera took the bouquet from him. "Adam? Take his coat and hang it up in the hall closet? Ram, you sit at this end of the table," she said and pulled the chair back for him. "What would you like to drink? Some wine, perhaps, an aperitif of bitters before dinner?"

He nodded and handed Adam his coat. "Either one would be fine, Mrs. Vorona." He sat down.

"Call me Lera."

"I can do that."

"Dare is going to love this bouquet!" Lera handed it back to him.

"I hope so."

Lera patted his shoulder. "Don't look so worried. She will."

Ram liked the petite dynamo. Adam dearly loved his wife and he could see why. She was more like a whirling dervish. He smiled inwardly at the image.

"Here she is!" Lera trilled out to him.

Dare halted at the cellar door that led off the kitchen. She had just brought up a bottle of red wine. "Hey, you found their place," she said, smiling at him and closing the door.

Ram stood up, the chair scraping the shining oak floor. "They do live out in the country," he admitted. His heart began to beat harder as he walked over to where she was. Lera took the bottle of wine from her, grinning like a fool, and whirled around and left. He saw a blush creeping up into Dare's high cheekbones as he handed her the bouquet. "After all those email photos of the flowers we happened upon when out on a mission, I thought having real ones would be better. These are for you." He handed the gold-wrapped bouquet to her. Their fingers met and Ram swore he got an electrical shock from their grazing contact. A look of surprise and then pleasure wreathed her smile as she accepted the huge bouquet.

"They're beautiful, Ram. Thank you." She buried her nose in the blooms. There were many lush, pink mallows, several golden sunflowers and small white chamomile daisies with big yellow centers, and many bright blue cornflowers to round out the grouping. The fragrance was exquisite and she inhaled it fully with appreciation.

He stood there, suddenly shy and pleased all at the same time. He'd never seen her blush before and it became her. The sky blue color of her eyes had always intrigued him and he hungrily absorbed her joy over his gift. Mostly, he was relieved she liked them. Relieved that she took them instead of refusing them. But Dare wasn't that kind of person. She'd take muffins from an Afghan horse and collect a gunny sack of them, and then give the manure to a local farmer who thought it was a great gift. He would take it and profusely thank her in Dari. Horse manure was used to help the plants in the field flourish and grow larger and increase the yield of corn or create larger heads of wheat for their family to eat. So, in Afghanistan, it was like receiving a bouquet of flowers.

"I wanted to get the autumn flowers of Ukraine for you," he began awkwardly, seeing how happy she was, her eyes sparkling. "I know how much you love this country and its people."

Dare sniffed and turned away, wiping her eyes with her free hand. She turned back, giving him a watery smile. "You are so thoughtful, Ram. I never expected this. Thank you."

He frowned, felt his heart fly open as he saw tears in her eyes start to gather again. "Flowers make you cry?"

She heard the teasing in his tone and surreptitiously wiped her tears away. "I don't know how you were able to find them at this time of year... That's what impresses me. How many hours did it take for you to locate them? I don't think these would be in florists' shops, do you?"

He had the good grace to manage a partial smile. Sticking his hands in the pockets of his black slacks, he murmured, "Well, my apartment is south of Kyiv, out in a rural farm area. There is a farm wife there who has a small florist business and the flowers come from her garden. Only Ukrainian flowers, by the way. She made up the bouquet for you."

"They are perfect," Dare managed, her voice husky.

"Here," Lera said, holding out a large crystal cut vase to her. "Let's give them water and set them on the table. They're all beautiful."

Ram took the vase and walked over to the kitchen sink and filled it. He felt a load slip off his shoulders. Earlier, he'd been afraid that Dare wouldn't like the bouquet or refuse it altogether. But she had not. The opposite had happened. And Lord help him, he almost threw his arms around her, wanting to crush her against him and hold her forever. In that moment, she looked vulnerable as never before to him. He realized belatedly that here with Lera and Adam's family, Dare was herself, not the combat medic on a black ops mission, rifle in hand. No, here she was herself and that

excited him beyond anything he'd ever expected. That
was a miracle of a gift he'd never expected.

How was he going to handle this new situation? He
was supposed to stay with Adam's family until Sunday afternoon. How?

Chapter Three

The kitchen was the heart of every Ukraine household and Ram silently reminisced about that as he awkwardly stood aside in the happy beehive of activity. Even Adam was in the mix, helping his wife with the setting of the long trestle table now decked out in a beautiful, crocheted tablecloth that he'd been told had been created by Lera's great-grandmother. It was a wedding gift to them when they'd gotten married. It reminded him of the sacredness of women who made such beautiful objects and then passed them on, generation after generation. There was a deep, heartfelt energy to it that embraced those who were present.

Dare was busy at one end of the counter, Lera on the other, getting the last-minute food preps ready. The girls were thrilled and excited with the gifts he'd given them and they'd run into the living room to check them out more closely. He'd discovered two apps on wildflowers of Ukraine and he knew from speaking to Dare that she was taking them out into the fields to look for and identify them. Dare had peeked at the app he'd given to them on a small computer tablet, and she jumped up and down with the girls, giving him a warm look of thanks for his thoughtfulness. Again, he'd felt heat rush into his face. This time, he didn't have a four-day growth of beard to hide it since he'd shaved, and showered, before his arrival.

"Hey," Adam called, waving to him from the entrance to the living room, "let's get out of the traffic and sit for about half an hour before dinner."

Ram nodded, happy to leave the kitchen area. It just brought back too many painful memories for him.

Adam had placed a small crystal glass of bitters on an antique table between two rocking chairs in the living room and gestured for him to come and sit down. "It's a beehive in there," he joked, smiling and sitting down.

Ram joined him. "Seriously," he agreed. He picked up the glass, sipping the bitters. The taste was tart, musty and he enjoyed it because this was an ancient custom in all of Europe to drink the herbal mixture before dinner so their digestion would be vastly improved, the meal made even more enjoyable as a result.

The girls had run to their bunk bedroom and Ram was sure they were having fun with their new botany flower app.

"Everything smells so good," Ram told his friend.

Inhaling, Adam closed his eyes for a moment and murmured, "I've often told Lera those kitchen smells are like perfume to me."

"Or to your stomach," Ram said, grinning a little.

Opening his eyes, Adam laughed, nodded and sipped

from his glass. "Most certainly." He grew somber, passing a look to Ram. "Did you get any more scoop on Russian activity at our border?"

"No, only that they're amassing about one hundred tanks." His mouth slashed downward. "I'd give my right arm to know where they are going to attack from. There are several major highways into Kyiv from that border area."

Adam scratched his head, his red hair short beneath his long fingers. "That's what worries me, Ram. Bucha is right on the most important highway artery that heads directly into the heart of Kyiv."

"Yes…" Ram noticed the deep worry in the man's blue eyes.

"I don't know what to do to tell Lera of my worries."

"Let's wait until we can get some more chatter traffic from the Russians. Sooner or later, they'll spill where they're going to attack us from because they're foolish and use their cell phones, which American intelligence picks up from their satellite feeds."

"You're right," he sighed, shaking his head. "I hate Putin…"

"I hate him more."

Adam gave him a questioning side-glance but said nothing.

Ram rocked gently, the kitchen cooking scents reminding him of another happy time in his life. Family, feasting and fun. That was how he experienced it growing up. There was nothing stronger among the Ukraine people than their bond with their family, their yearly ceremonies, supporting and caring for their entire village, town or city or the love they held for this largest country in Europe. He purposely blotted out the hatred that ate at him daily regarding Putin. He was a monster unleashed and Ram knew just how violent and heartless he really was. Wrestling with all those crisis emotions he kept to himself, he forced himself to turn to something happy: Dare.

He'd been sent to the USA with his team off and on the last six months after coming out of Afghanistan once and for all. He had kept tabs on Dare's assignment in Lviv, teaching advanced and accelerated combat field medicine techniques to their medics. His own home was in a small village south of Kyiv, a good hour's drive from the center of the city where the military HQ was situated.

He knew Dare lived in the heart of the city, in an apartment in a high-rise a few blocks from the central military buildings. But he never contacted her face-to-face, instead continuing to send her flower emails from time to time. The last six months he'd not been able to, his entire team in the USA and under intense military training with weapons they would use to push back the coming Russian attack. He wanted so much more with her, but now, the war loomed. Just when he'd talked himself into trying to create an opening, a dialogue with her about how he felt personally about her, it was destroyed.

Things had changed within him, however. And maybe…just maybe? He'd gotten the courage to see her in person, and that somehow…and God only knew how…he would let her know how he felt. Ram wasn't sure what her reaction would be because he'd always kept that unscalable wall between them.

Now? All that had changed. Closing his eyes for a moment, leaning his head back on the rocker, he wanted this war to go away, to never happen. He wanted that opening he'd planned on, hoped for, to be the moment he could let her know how much he wanted her personally in his life. Was he too late? Should he even try? She was back in his team. The last place he wanted her. The last…

"Dinner is ready," Lera sang at the entrance to the living room.

LERA PLACED EVERYONE at the table. Dare wasn't sure she was happy about being next to Ram, but it would have been embarrassing to everyone if she'd said she wanted to sit elsewhere. So, she sat. Giving him a soft smile as she sat down, the pink linen napkin unfolding as she placed it in her lap, she said, to him, "Doesn't this food look good or what?"

He nodded. "Smells as good as I'm sure it will taste, too."

Her spirits lifted a tiny bit. When he'd entered the kitchen with Adam, he looked positively torn up about something, but she could only begin to guess what it might be about. With everyone seated, they all held hands, bowed their heads and Adam gave the family prayer. Ram's fingers were work worn and heavily calloused, and hers, not as much. Her heart leaped with need of him when he gently enfolded her hand into his, holding it lightly. It reminded her of a man gently holding a baby. She knew his strength; he was built tall and solid, but he held her fingers as if she might break at a moment's notice. There had been so few times that they'd actually touched one another, except to settle a pack, hand a clip of ammunition or grasp a loose strap that might make noise and give their position away and tuck it in where it wouldn't make a sound.

THE GIRLS FACED THEM, and Lera and Adam sat at each end of the table. The children were giggling and covering their mouths with their hands, still excited about the tablets that Ram had gifted them. The first course was minestrone soup with Italian sausage. Adam filled the soup dishes and passed them around. The girls, however, had much smaller soup dishes. Ram envied their innocence. In his business and life, there had been very little of that. But he enjoyed the children's reactions and smiled inwardly.

He was acutely aware of Dare at his right arm. The table was long enough to give them ample breathing room, but sometimes his elbow would accidentally brush her left arm. It was Lera and Adam who kept up the table chatter for the most part. His whole world encircled Dare. Was she even attracted to him? His stomach clenched momentarily, afraid of that answer. She had never shown any flirtatious actions toward him, ever. She joked routinely with the other men of his team, but never with him. Why? And yet, the men of his team brutally teased him from time to time, and vice versa. He finished the soup. There would be a salad next, and then the main course, dessert and coffee or tea to follow.

"Eh, Ram," Lera sang, waving her fork in his direction. "Did you put your suitcase in that second bedroom down the hall?"

"Uh," he replied and frowned. "No, it's still in the car."

Adam chuckled. "What? You're afraid if Lera's cooking was bad you'll make your escape tonight? Never to be seen here again?" He laughed heartily. Everyone knew Lera was a fabulous cook. People in their village always begged for her pastries, pies and cakes to be made by her when they held a festival or a ceremony.

"I'll bring it in after dinner," he managed, spooning the potato salad onto his plate as the bowl was passed to him by Dare. Their fingers met. He hungrily absorbed the momentary contact. And again, her cheeks flushed. Was that a good sign? Or a bad one? If only he could know. "I'll get the suitcase in after dinner," he promised Lera.

November 3

IT WAS DARK and quiet in the household when Ram silently got up, dressed in his pajamas and winter robe and walked down the hall without being heard. Everyone had gone to bed at 2300, 11:00 p.m. The girls had gone earlier. Dare's bedroom was up ahead on the left and he wanted to make sure he didn't make any sounds to awaken her. She had looked beautiful to him throughout dinner and then everyone enjoyed their aperitif wine in the living room afterward.

The girls had crowded around his feet with their new tablets begging him to help them with the software so they could learn how to better navigate the app and they could see all the rest of the flowers. Ram had worked patiently with them, getting each tablet set up, and then the girls oohed and aahed over the colorful photos. They would hurry around the living room showing everyone in a rocker or overstuffed chair. The wood fireplace sent warmth throughout the rooms. Earlier, Adam had put on some quiet classical music in the background and Ram enjoyed the low lighting, the flames of the fire like dancing shadows throughout the room. To his surprise, Dare had chosen to sit with him on a loveseat, but he didn't say anything one way or another.

So when was the right time and place? He felt impatient, desperately wanting to have a quiet conversation with her. As he stepped from the hall into the living room, his attention was drawn to the kitchen. There was a slight noise, but he wasn't sure what that meant. Keeping his presence unknown as he walked to the entrance, his heart pounded briefly. There was Dare in her fuzzy one-piece flannel pj's with a cream-colored lambswool robe over it.

"Oh!"

"Sorry," he murmured, holding up his hands, giving her an apologetic look.

She pressed her hand against her heart. "You scared me!"

Ram had the good grace to try to smile a little. "I didn't mean to. I'm sorry, Dare. What are you doing up?" It was 0200. Outside, the rain was furiously pelting against the windows. The wind was still coming and going in huge gusts through the trees surrounding the home.

"Couldn't sleep," she muttered, frowning. "I ate too much. I love good food and Lera's is just the best." She touched her tummy. "I was getting another glass of bitters to help with my digestion."

"Go ahead," he urged. "I overate, too. She's a great cook." He sat down at the table, watching her. Every movement since he'd known her was filled with grace. She never made any jerking or jabbing movements and maybe it was a feminine-masculine thing. But he'd seen her under fire on too many missions and she could shoot as good as anyone on his team.

"Do you want a glass of bitters?"

"No. I've had a lifetime of bitterness, I don't need extra."

She hesitated, then gave him a long, momentary look, and then poured the bitters from the crystal glassware into a smaller awaiting glass. "Where did that comment come from?" she asked gently, turning, glass in hand, and sitting at the end of the table where Lera had sat earlier.

He shrugged. "Haven't you seen how some people's lives fall into different categories, Dare? Some lead very happy lives where everything seems to go right for them. They get the breaks, the opportunities. And then there is another class of people who scavenge for every penny, every step in their life. They work hard, much harder than others, and in the end they become very successful, respected people."

"What about this bitter class? How do you see them?"

His mouth twisted and he looked away for a moment. "Oh… They lead bitter lives. They might have had a terrible childhood or a really good one, but then something devastating happens to them and everything turns bitter and it's a dark tunnel that never ends. There's no daylight at the end of it, no hope, and there's no happy ending for those kinds of people."

She studied him in the silence. "So? Which class are you in?"

Ram shrugged, wanting to tell her everything but it was so damned hard to even begin because he had no hope. "What about you?" he parried. "I'll bet you're in the happy-life group." He saw her eyes change and her mouth thinned.

"I'm in the bitter class, Ram."

Shocked, he stared at her. "You?"

Sitting back, Dare felt his powerful emotions and the utter disbelief in his expression. His eyes narrowed. So? He saw her as happy? Or the struggling camp, instead?

"We've never been personal with one another," she began in a low tone, holding his intense gaze. "Do you really want to know who I am? Warts and all? Because for two years, I never felt that you were really interested in me except for my skill levels. Our communication was strictly professional and on an as-needed basis only."

Ram wiped his mouth. He was sweating. He had to drop this damnable shield he lived behind if he was to unveil how he really felt toward her. He felt helpless, a feeling he stopped when his life was murdered and he had to start all over. But he was feeling it now. "I'm not going to lie to you," he began, voice little more than a growl. "I could not be personal with you in Afghanistan."

"Well, that's true," she said, "but there was no camaraderie between us like you had with the men of the team, either, Ram."

He gave a nod, seeing the hurt reflected in her eyes as well as the question: Why? "It was me," he admitted tiredly, wiping his hands on his thighs. "I wanted to. I mean, I really did, but I was afraid."

She settled back in the chair. "Afraid of what? Me?"

"Sounds kind of silly now, doesn't it?" The derision in his voice was aimed at himself, not her. He saw her eyes lighten, her mouth losing some of that tense line as she held his gaze. "I think part of it was your confidence and fearlessness, Dare. You didn't scare at all, no matter if we were in a firefight, or if you were exposing yourself in order to rescue Artur when he was shot, and I was amazed, like the rest of the team, at your raw, fierce courage."

Snorting, she muttered, "Oh, I was scared, Ram. Just as scared as the rest of you. But you have to remember, I'm combat medic. I know that I'll be the one to crawl toward our wounded teammate under a hail of fire. The likelihood of getting shot was not only real but happens a lot. So far, I've been lucky, but that's just it. My day will come when I won't be so lucky."

Scowling, he growled, "I don't want you to take risks like that...not now, not ever, moving forward."

Relaxing a little, she finished off her bitters and set the crystal on the table. "You don't become a medic for yourself, Ram, you become one for your team, no matter who they are or the danger they are in. You know very well medics will risk their lives every day. And that's not going to change with me when I join your team again."

The silence grew.

Finally, Ram muttered, "I knew you'd say that."

"So why do you think I'm not in the bitter class?"

He was almost relieved by the change of topic. Pushing around in the chair, he said, "Because you don't behave like a person who is."

"I see. What class do you see yourself in, then?"

"Bitter."

"Could you say a little more?"

He managed a twisted smile. "You first?"

Dare nodded, studying him. "I fit your description of bitter, but maybe I'm in more than one class. My mother wrapped me in a blanket and placed me on the steps of a firehouse where a fireman would find me as a newborn baby."

Blinking, he rasped, "You were abandoned?"

"Yes. I have no memory of it, of course. Three months later I was adopted by a Ukrainian couple who had been in the USA for ten years. My adopted father, Panas Mazur, is a world-class cardiologist and had been lured to come do his research and work at the Cleveland Clinic in Cleveland, Ohio. My mother, Maria Mazur, is a high school science teacher in that city. They had dual citizenship with Ukraine and the USA when they adopted me. I never knew I was adopted and I was very much loved and cared for by them. It wasn't until I was fourteen when they sat me down to tell me the rest of my life story."

"That," he struggled, "was almost the worst thing I can think of happening to a person. I'm sorry. It must make you feel very bad sometimes."

"It did at first, but by the time I was eighteen, I'd reconciled myself to the situation, Ram. I didn't let it stop me from doing what I wanted to do with my life. I still don't know who my mother is, but I live with it. The tremendous love Maria and Panas gave me growing up I think did a lot of healing inside me. I didn't feel thrown away or left to die. I've always believed that if you're supposed to live, you'll be protected and able to go on and achieve your dreams."

He sat there, allowing her situation to move through him without slamming the door shut on his emotions regarding it. She was so sure of herself, never questioning who she was, or her dream she wanted to come true. "You're truly an amazing person," he managed, emotions coloring his voice. "I would *never* have guessed you were orphaned."

"It could have turned out to be bitter," she admitted, "but the love lavished upon me by my adopted parents made all the difference, Ram. Love healed me in ways I couldn't even imagine. And they love me fiercely to this day." She smiled softly, lifting her gaze to the ceiling for a moment. "I don't know if it's because they are Ukrainian. Or the tight-knit family, the extended family they have, that has made them this way, but I sure soaked up their love and healed."

"That is an incredible story," he rasped, "and very uplifting, not depressing."

"Oh, I would get depressed sometimes, Ram. I had ups and downs, but that left me early on because my parents would go home to Lviv, Ukraine, where their entire extended family lives, and I absorbed even more of their family's affection for me." She sighed and smiled faintly. "I was the most loved being in the world as far as I was concerned. Later, as I matured, I understood it was the Ukraine family way of living together that was the safety net that helped save me from feeling like I wasn't worth keeping. All the greater family's love was showered upon me like a protective bubble, and as far as I'm concerned, it made the difference."

"I often wondered why you spoke the Ukraine language so fluently," he said more to himself than her. "You have a natural way of speaking it and there are few who would be able to guess that you are an American."

"I grew up with it," she said. "Maria taught me Russian, also." She gave him a wry look. "That might come in handy next year when we're out in the field."

He grunted and nodded. "Russians murder, rape

and torture their enemies and they will destroy the civilian populace as fast as they will us in the military. Unless we accidentally listen in on a local Russian radio call or our comms pick up cell phone chatter between themselves. That information could come in handy and we would pass it on to our intel people."

"The Afghan people fought them for years and they won. Russia backed out."

"They've bit off the wrong country, again," was all Ram would say.

She tilted her head. "I like that we're really talking human-to-human with one another. This is a first."

"It is, isn't it?"

"Is it painful?"

He grinned at her teasing. "No. Liberating, maybe…"

"In what way, Ram?"

Shrugging, he said, "I've been wanting to have conversations like this with you ever since I met you, Dare," and he held her shocked expression.

Silence.

"I've never known you to not have a comeback," he teased her gently. She was giving him a strange, confused look.

"Why now?" she choked.

He looked away for a moment, then lifted his chin, holding her bewildered stare. "It wouldn't have been appropriate in Afghanistan."

Nodding, she whispered, "Yes, you're right, of course." Lips flexing, she asked, "Why now?"

"I was waiting for the right opportunity, Dare. I have no say in where our team is sent, but when we came back here, I thought we'd be here awhile, but we weren't. We were sent to America for six months of further training. We got back here the past week. I was still hoping you were here, and you were. I thought you were in Lviv, unaware of your assignment to teach in Kyiv." He held up his scarred hands. "When we came back, my CO gave me your orders to team up with you again and I couldn't believe it. You were here, in Kyiv."

She gave him an amused look. "Why couldn't you believe it?"

Shaking his head, he muttered, "I'm a bitter person, Dare. Nothing ever works out for me. Not the way I want. Not ever. Getting sent back here to Kyiv I thought was my opportunity to try and forge some sort of a personal relationship with you over time. Then, we spent half a year in the USA. And add to this mix, Russia is going to attack our country sometime early next year. Three things to stop me from wanting to have a different…better relationship with you if you wanted one with me."

"And yet," she murmured, "here you are."

"Is this offer one-sided?" Holding his breath, he saw her grow thoughtful, turning the stem of the crystal slowly around between her slender fingers. Fingers that had sewn the injured people back together. She was a lifesaver in so many ways, Ram thought. A lifesaver to him, as well. His stomach clenched as the silence grew heavily between them. Unable to stand it, he uttered, "Look, if you're in a relationship—"

"I'm not."

"Oh."

"And you?"

He raised a brow.

"Hey, what is good for the goose, Kozak, is good for the gander where I come from."

A grin leaked out. "You've always told us how you felt about something. Why stop now?" He saw her blue eyes deepen in color.

"Honesty is the best policy. It's a good ole American saying."

"America has some really interesting slang." He studied her, seeing her arch her back, giving him that demanding look she could give someone. "I am not in a relationship," he admitted. Dare appeared relieved. Could it be true? That perhaps she liked him in a romantic way? Just a little bit? His heart thudded once to underscore that possibility.

"I know absolutely nothing about you, Ram. Only your being our captain and that you're a damned good leader and tactician."

"Have we crossed the Rubicon?" he wondered.

"I don't know. What do you consider a relationship? It has many definitions."

Wariness was in her husky tone and eyes. Ram couldn't blame her. What was he offering her? A bitter person. Who would ever want one of those bad-luck souls around? He sure wouldn't. Why did he hope that she *did* want him around? What could he offer her? What would she think of his past? She'd glibly talked about her past as if it were nothing, but he knew it was monumental. One didn't get thrown away by their mother and not feel the lifelong sting of abandonment. Still, she didn't act like it, always confident in herself and her abilities and skills.

She was not a braggart, nor was she arrogant. Instead, she was quietly skilled at saving lives. He'd always admired and respected her for that. The fact she'd been abandoned, for whatever the mother's reasoning, was a scar she'd carry all her life and Ram was sure it would never disappear. Just as the scars he wore would do the same. There was no escaping that kind of deep, grinding pain that might soften a little over time. He understood he'd die with his, as she would die with hers.

"We have a war staring us in the face," he said heavily. "And we have to work together again in a team where there can be no personal ties to one another."

"And that's why I asked why you would want any kind of relationship. The timing is bad, Ram."

"I learned my lesson the first time with you," he rasped, feeling as if he were going to lose her before he ever had a chance to know her heart, her soul. "I kept putting it off in Afghanistan. I am an officer. You are an enlisted person. The military does not bless such a union. And then, when the US Army hauled you out of my team to assign you to teach in Lviv, I realized all my planning was for nothing."

"Real life intercedes all the time. We know that as black ops. All we can do is expect change, Ram."

"Have you ever had a deep relationship in your life?"

It was an odd question to ask, but she saw how serious he was about it. "A few, back in college. Once I entered the Army and made Special Forces, I knew I couldn't do both. I either focused on one or another." She hitched one shoulder, a wryness to her tone. "I figured if I was able to make it there, to get into their world-class medical combat program, that later I'd have time for a serious relationship down the road."

"And how did that work out for you?"

"It didn't. I was tops in my class and I was one of the few chosen to enter the advanced surgical field combat training, and I jumped at it. I think my dad had a real influence on me regarding it as I grew up. He would show me a stethoscope, an oximeter, and taught me how to take a blood pressure reading with a cuff. He taught me how to stitch a wound closed with an orange and some dental floss. I was hungry to learn anything medical. When I was eight years old, for Christmas, they gave me a child's physician bag, and I was over the moon." She smiled fondly. "I've always loved medicine and helping people. My dad saved so many lives with the skills he had in his hands and with his training. I wanted to do the same thing. When I was twelve, they sent me to a summer camp for children in Switzerland that was all about beginning medical training. It was the best summer I'd had because it was there that I focused on what I really wanted to do in life."

"To join the Army? Become a medic?"

"Yes, to work in the field of medicine in some way."

"BUT WHY THE MILITARY? You had a family that could easily have paid for your premed education at some of the finest medical schools in America. Yes?"

"Yes, my dad wanted me to go to Harvard. But I wanted adventure, Ram. I didn't want to sit in premed classes for four years and pound memorization into my brain. I wanted to be in the field, hands-on, learn on the job and save lives. When I was seventeen, my father talked the local fire chief into allowing me to become an EMT, emergency medical technician. It was a fourteen-week course and I passed it with flying colors. That's when one of the instructors, the assistant chief, who had been a Special Forces combat field medic, told me the stories of the lives he saved in the field. I knew without a doubt that was exactly what I wanted to do. In fact, he contacted a general, talked to him and wrote a wonderful reference letter to get me into their program."

"You're a brave soul, Dare Mazur."

She shrugged. "My poor parents were worried by my decision. There were three of us girls in that class. We all made the cut. One went into communications and the other became a weapons expert."

"And you became the medic?"

"Yep, and I loved it. I really had no time for an affair or ongoing relationship with a guy. All my time was hands-on learning, which I'm very good at. I don't do well learning by book or taking online computer classes. I like being in the thick of things, kinesthetic training, hands-on and then it sticks with me. I remember it."

"I'm sure your parents continue to be very worried for you."

She sighed. "Yes, a lot of worry when I was ordered to go to Afghanistan."

"What about now? They're in America. You are here in Ukraine. The Army now needs us to stay in-country to help us fight for our democracy. They must still be very worried about that."

She became glum, holding the crystal stem between her fingers. "They are beside themselves with worry. I haven't told them about the orders to go into your team, Ram. They were expecting me to come home to the US and be safe."

"Any parent would worry about their child in a situation like this," he agreed. "When are you going to break this news to them?"

She gave him a weary look. "I don't know yet... They realize I'm in the Army and I can't just walk away and go live in Cleveland with them. I just signed back up for another six-year hitch. I thought I'd be in Kyiv teaching during my enlistment...not out on the battlefield again."

Silence fell over them. He roused himself and he sat up, holding her sad gaze. "So where does that leave us? What do you want to do about this?" Again, his stomach clenched. Ram tried to steel himself against the obvious answer that he knew would come from her.

She smiled slightly. "I like the idea of a friendship with you. That is a relationship. What did you have in mind?"

He rubbed his jaw. "I like the idea of a friendship. I want to earn the right to be your friend."

She smiled softly. "That feels good to me. Why not come with us and the girls tomorrow morning? We're going to be hunting for rose hips and Lera is going to teach me how to make jelly out of them."

"Sounds exciting," he deadpanned, a slight lift of the corners of his mouth. "I'd like to go with you." Hope infused him. She hadn't turned him down. She didn't say no. Friendship? It was better than nothing. And perhaps, over time, it could turn into something deeper and more long-lasting.

Chapter Four

November 3

Anna and Sophia were dressed warmly on the cool November morning after the storm had passed. The ground was wet, the grass long, yellowed and tangling around their rubber-booted feet as Dare aimed the happy little group toward a hedgerow of bushes ahead of them. Dare looked up, the sky still filled with low, ragged-looking clouds, the end of the front still coming through, lots of patches of light blue sky here and there. The air was crisp and she inhaled it deeply, loving the scent of the musky earth after the sweet smell of rain had lavished the soil. Most of the trees that ringed the property, a large square of ten acres, were losing their colorful leaves. The wild rosebushes grew between the trees, many of them ten to twelve feet tall. They were very old, well established, and even at this distance, she could see the bright red rose hips that reminded her of red bulb decorations that were hung on a Christmas tree.

Glancing to her right, she saw Ram walking a few feet away from her, looking around, a habit of being in black ops. The cries of ravens erupted suddenly, and she saw a buck and three does running from one area to another. Right now, it was mating season and she enjoyed seeing the wildlife that were more intent on that than being seen by humans. Smiling, with Anna on her left and Sophia on her right, she said, "Did you see them?" She pointed toward the deer.

"Oh, yes!" Anna cried, "How pretty!"

"They're staring at us!" Sophia said.

"I think they're surprised we're here," Dare agreed. She carried two five-gallon buckets in her hands and Ram carried the other two.

The deer took off, white tails in the air, disappearing once more into the woods.

"Tell me again what we're doing this morning?" Ram asked.

Dare suppressed a smile. He'd overslept this morning and Adam had to rouse him so he could leave on time with them. "Rose hips. Lera's mother was a sixth-generation herbalist. They used the rose hips as a tea or tincture throughout the fall, winter and spring to cure colds and flu."

"I like them!" Anna said, jumping up and down, throwing her arms into the air.

"I do, too!" Sophia said, not wanting to be left out of the commentary.

"What do you like best about them?" Dare asked the six-year-old.

"I like the jelly! I like lots and lots of it on toast with butter!"

"Sounds good," Ram added, smiling a little at the child whose cheeks were a rosy red.

"Rose hip jam and jelly are a forever food here in Ukraine," Dare said to him. "Surely you had it in your family?"

Ram grimaced and said, "Yeah, I suppose we did." He wasn't going there today. He was trying to learn how to be a friend to Dare. He had no idea how to go about it, however. Men were friends. Women? Well, in his life they were never friends. Lovers? Yes. But a friend? He was having trouble separating sex from friendship, the need to love Dare versus what friends would do instead. He never had this problem before because all his friends were male.

"Did you ever go out with your mother or grand-mother and pick them in the late fall like this?"

He squirmed inwardly. "I really don't have such a memory..." he answered, purposefully vague. Feeling guilty more than ever because yesterday early morning Dare had opened up her private life to him, sharing events through her childhood. He'd been a thirsty, hungry wolf for just such information from her because it helped him understand her. He'd always wondered what made her tick and now he knew: her medical doctor father had a powerful influence over her, but in truth, she had an inner love and drive to be in the field of medicine, anyway. It helped explain to him why she was so devoted to her career, why she took risks that all combat medics would take sooner or later—and live to tell about it.

Ram knew he was super protective, like a father

with his children, of his team. The responsibility weighed heavily on him, without relief, but he didn't care because he was a Ukrainian patriot and would do anything for his "family" and his country. He saw the questioning in her gaze as they walked with his non-answer. He didn't like doing that to her, but with two energetic young ones with them, it was not an appropriate place to speak to her on more personal terms. They were approaching one end of a half-mile-long hedgerow of wild rosebushes and he could see the red rose hips everywhere among the leaves.

The girls surged ahead, squealing with excitement, their hands in gloves so that their small fingers wouldn't keep getting poked with the tiny needlelike thorns. The wind was chilly and he'd pulled up the sheepskin collar of his jacket to protect the back of his neck.

Dare was well prepared, a purple knit cap on her short, dark hair. A muffler around her neck, the ends tied at her throat. He remembered when she'd first come to the team, her hair had literally been halfway down her back. It didn't take long for her to figure out that the long strands would get caught in everything and slow her response time, plus cause a lot of other issues when they were getting shot at. He recalled after that mission she'd asked Adam to chop it all off, and his second-in-command looked anguished over doing it. Dare hadn't. She was relieved to get it out of the way. Much to his surprise, she gave the shorn locks to an Afghan woman who weaved it for an older woman who was going bald, and she created a wig of sorts out of it for her.

Afghan women were famous for making something out of nothing. Dare had taken her locks to the village and given them to the weaver, who set to work. Those two years they were there, that particular village always invited them for feasts and ceremonies after that. It had been one of the few positive bright spots in their time in that war-torn, starving country.

"We'll start here," Dare told him, setting the buckets down at the end of the row. "Ram, if the rose hip is green, yellow or orange? It's not ripe, so let it stay on the bush. Just pick the bright red ones."

"There's all colors on this one," he said, looking it up and down.

"A Christmas tree with light bulbs, for sure," she said, smiling over at him.

He felt his heart thud once, privy to that sweet smile of hers that flowed through him. Dare was happy. He could see it in her dancing blue gaze, the tilt of the corners of her soft mouth curving upward. Managing a slight smile, he said, "Strange Christmas tree, but you're right." Right now, she was setting each bucket about two meters apart for the girls, as well as for themselves.

Each child claimed a bucket and swiftly began to collect the ripe rose hips with a blur of tiny hands in motion. She placed the third bucket, hers, between her booted feet, going to work.

Ram said, "I'll go this way," and he pointed to his right. He halted and for a moment watched the little girls as they started at the top, as high as they could reach, and then came down vertically until they were bent over, getting the last of the rose hips at the bottom of the bush they'd been assigned. Then, they'd move a few inches, and start at the top and work their way down another row. He mimicked their way of doing things.

The sun peeked out, warming him and brightening the land around them. He felt a kind of peace descend over him with Dare and the children nearby. It brought back a lot of sweet memories from his early boyhood.

"What are we going to do with all these seeds when we get back to their home?" he wondered.

"Oh, we have a lot to do when we get them home, Ram. It's a process. First, we wash them under running, cold water and take off any thing that doesn't belong on them. We have to make sure there's no bird poop on them, either."

He laughed, and it felt good. "I never really thought about that angle of it." He could see the devilry dancing in her eyes, his smile broadening. "What else? This is really entertaining."

"Every berry is investigated completely, believe me. You don't want to see that rose hip ending up with something white or gray on it, or insect parts sticking out of it, in your jar of jam or jelly."

He chuckled. "Okay, I get your point. What else do you do with them?"

She reached above her head, expertly picking off the ripe seeds, but leaving the rest and not damaging the branch they were found on. "We will freeze all of them over night."

"Why is that?"

"We have to open each one up with a sharp knife the next morning, cutting them in half, and if they're frozen, it's just so much easier to do. We have to be sure to scrape and collect all the seeds inside the hip, and also, each seed has lots of tiny little hairs on it. We have to scrape the inner part of the hip clean so they're all removed. If you don't, those hairs prick you. The inside of your mouth will becoming highly irritated and itch like crazy."

He began plucking the hips, not as fast or as nimbly as Dare, who obviously had lots of experience doing this. Looking down the row, Ram saw the girls going Mach 3 with their red hair on fire, their small hands a blur of speed, the constant drop, drop, drop of the hips into their bucket situated between their feet.

"That's a lot of work." He looked down at his bucket, the bottom covered. "I must have picked fifty or so already. You three are way ahead of me."

She snorted. "We'll do *thousands* of them before this is all over."

He gave her a teasing, evil look. "Now I see why you wanted me to come this weekend."

"We need every able-bodied person we can find to help us. This is the best time of year to get the rose hips. We aren't the only ones doing it," she said and tilted her head to the right.

Ram saw at least five families of men, women and children coming their way with buckets in hand. "The whole town's coming? What is this? Rose Hip Week-end? Is that why Adam asked me to stay over? He never mentioned *this*."

Snickering, Dare said, "Adam is sneaky, you know that, Ram. Those folks who are coming will be standing two meters apart, just like we're doing. That's your plot or space you pick within. Don't wander into someone else's territory, okay?"

"Wouldn't think of it," he said, lifting a hand in hello at the approaching families. Everyone was merry. There was a lot of laughter and joking as they got to work down the row of rosebushes. "So? Everyone makes jam and jelly out of these rose hips?"

Nodding, Dare dropped a handful into her buckets, glad to have her thick leather gloves on. "The ones that are orange colored will get red in the next several days. Then, you'll see another group of families coming down to pick them when that happens. It's an annual village affair, for sure. Everyone will get enough."

"Adam once said that Lera was an herbalist?"

"Yes. She comes from a long line of women in her family, the information passed down from one generation to the next. She's been helping me to become more aware about herbs since my assignment in Kyiv, and I stay at their home on most weekends. I get to watch her making her herb infusions, decoctions, salves, ointments and teas for the people of the village. There are ten women in the village who are what we call the wise women. They're the ones who know the plants, and they know which ones are medicinal and how to make them so they help a human or animal. I love it because for me, it's a more natural kind of medicine. I like learning about the plants because they can be used out in the field if I don't have anything in my pack."

Nodding, Ram was impressed. "Does Lera have anything for sore knees?"

Dare made a face. "Oh, yeah. Tell me which of our team doesn't have sore joints. In our business, our elbows, knees and hip joints take a beating."

"Your knees, also?"

"Yes." She held up a handful of rose hips. "One of the many medicinal areas these little red seeds help is joint inflammation."

He stared at the innocuous rose hips. "Seriously?"

"Yes. When I came here from Afghanistan I asked Lera for something because my joints were really barking at me. She made a tea out of the rose hips and sent me home with a canister of the powder. I was to make one cup of tea and drink it every day."

"What did it do for you?"

"Within three days, the pain in my knees stopped, the inflammation and swelling were starting to reduce, which was a huge relief. Two weeks into a cup a day? My knees were like new and the swelling was completely gone. Lera had said that rose hips are very gentle and anyone can drink it as a tea. It's a very active medicinal herb and is superb when used by people like us, or folks who have osteoarthritis or rheumatoid arthritis."

"I think I'd better start giving these red berries a

lot more respect," he murmured, looking thoughtfully into his half-filled bucket.

"You can drink a cup of tea daily, or use the jam or jelly on your toast every morning, and it will do the same thing. Lots of different ways to take it. I make up capsules with the powder and will take two of them a day if I don't have time to make the tea on some mornings before I teach classes."

"Who'd have thought a little red seed like this could do so much good for us?"

"Roger that," she said, looking at her bucket, "because medicinal herbs are so important. They can save a life, and if you really want to get technical about it. It was medical herbs since humans arrived here on Earth that saved our species and allowed us to flourish and populate the planet. We were a plant-and-herb-taking population until just recently, the past hundred years or so if you want to think about it. Herbs work. The proof is in the fact there's a huge human population on Earth."

"How else do these unsung seeds help us?"

"If you take four grams a day of the rose hip powder for six weeks it can reduce your cardiovascular risk. It lowers the systolic blood pressure and also lowers your cholesterol levels."

"That's really amazing." He studied the red seed again, impressed.

"And…if that isn't enough? This little seed will take on inflammation anywhere in our body and science is now realizing how deadly that particular condition is for all of us."

"So, the people here in this village drink the tea daily?"

"Yes. The men especially like it because they get sore joints from doing a lot of hard, physical labor."

"Too bad we didn't have this around in Afghanistan," he grumbled. "We sure could have used it."

"Isn't that the truth," she agreed.

"It's kind of a super-medicinal herb?"

"Yes and no. There are a number of medicinal herbs that have a lot of areas of application. Lera knows *all* of them. She's a walking encyclopedia. I keep an herb journal with me, and when I'm here on weekends, we'll sit down at least once or twice and she'll give me information on an herb that grows around Bucha that she uses."

"Do herbs have any vitamin or minerals in them?" he wondered.

"Plants are super good in a nutritional sense." She straightened and opened her gloved hand, ticking off some of the benefits. "Like the rose hips? They have vitamin C, calcium, magnesium, potassium, beta-carotene, quercetin, tocopherols and lycopene. They are a very rich source of so many nutrients that humans need. And people in the USA are severely magnesium deficient because that mineral is no longer found in our soil because of the way the farmers tilled and manage their land hundreds of years earlier. Magnesium helps us combat stress, and if you're deficient, you may have insomnia, broken sleep and it just gets worse over time." She held up a fat red rose hip. "If you would just take a cup of tea a day? You're helping your body in so many positive ways."

He thought for a moment. "You're right…" He gave her a praising look. She grinned and went back to work.

"Race to fill up my bucket before you do yours…"

"You're on," he growled, and started working a Mach three with his hair on fire.

November 7

DARE HURRIED ACROSS the street and headed toward the military complex building in central Kyiv. She checked her watch. Feeling stressed because she had been late meeting the people in the human resources department, ending her teaching duties at a certain date, had taken more time than she thought.

She reached the top-secret area where she knew Ram's team was going to meet today. Going down a brightly lit, highly waxed hall far underground, she found the conference room and opened the door. Stepping in, she saw Ram standing near the front of the room, the rest of the men seated at the long oval oak table. Each one had a laptop in front of him. Luckily, she had hers in her backpack. She grinned and lifted her hand, saying, "And here I thought I'd never see any of you guys again!"

A roar of welcome went up and every man stood, coming over to slap her back or hug her or grab her hand and shake it in welcome. Dare hadn't expected this kind of reaction, but she was happy to see the team she'd left two years earlier. Off to one side, she saw Ram standing, watching them, face unreadable, although his eyes glittered. A couple of men and Leonid, who was a mechanic and artillery expert, lifted her off her feet, squeezing the breath out of her, a fierce welcome from someone she loved dearly like a long-lost brother, and who had always been super protective of her because she was a woman.

As soon as she was put down, Borysko, a blond-haired, blue-eyed and bearded six-footer, lifted her up and twirled her around, grinning and welcoming her "home" and saying that he'd missed her terribly and was so glad she was back with them.

Blinking back tears, she saw these men as her brothers, most of them around her age. They escorted her to the table, showing her the seat they'd saved for her, a top-secret laptop already open and waiting for her. She noted that Ram would be sitting next to her and that Adam took his seat on the other side of his leader. The table rocked with lots of questions, answers and laughter, not to mention black humor jokes. It was a wonderful welcome. All of them looked older, but she'd been gone for two years from the team, and she knew the stress of constant engagement and combat, which all black ops dealt with. They'd earned every line in their faces, old before their time.

The door opened and suddenly the room quieted. Dare saw two intelligence officers, a man and woman, crisply enter the room. They were majors, so that meant they were bringing a lot of highly classified intel to them. Everyone became seated. Ram sat down and gave her a brief nod of hello. Everyone faced forward toward the intel officers at the front of the long table. Dare pulled out her pen and notebook, something she was never without at these meetings. The laptop in front of her jumped to life and it was connected with the officers' tablets at the front of the room. Feeling like she was settling into an old, well-known groove, she listened to them begin to talk about the coming war with Russia.

The hours had moved swiftly. By the time the intel officers had laid it all out for them, it was 1500, 3:00 p.m. Dare's head swam with consternation. When would she tell her parents that she was a part of Ram's team once more? They knew what that meant. She had put them through two years of anxiety hell, wondering if she would be wounded or killed in action on any given day of the week in Afghanistan.

The last weekend at Adam and Lera's home was 180 degrees different from today. Every face in the room was now grim. She felt Ram's energy, although his back was to her, all his attention on the intelligence briefing. It was comforting to have him close to her right now. This was different. This was their country that would be attacked. He'd always given her that sense of safety even out on missions. She wondered if his men felt the same way, fairly sure that they did.

"Dismissed," the woman major told them, shutting down her tablet and placing it into a brown calf leather briefcase at the end of the conference table.

Everyone stood, little being said until the intel officers had departed. Then, Dare heard the murmuring among the team members. Most of all, she searched Adam's very dire-looking face. He seemed shocked to Dare, but why wouldn't he be? One of the main routes into Kyiv was right through the village of Bucha, where they lived. The intel people left nothing unsaid about Russians and their lack of mercy and never following the Geneva Conventions if they took Ukrainians prisoner. Worse? The woman drilled into them, her dark eyes filled with warning, when she said the Russians would go through a civilian village and they would rape the girls and women and kill the men, and any young man of soldier age would be tortured, shot and buried in an unmarked grave. It turned Dare's stomach and she wrestled with worry over Adam's family.

"Hey," Ram said, approaching her, "you ready to go?"

Shaken, she nodded, saying nothing. She followed him out of the room after saying goodbye to the team. The men would meander out of the room at their own pace. He walked at her shoulder.

"This way," he urged her quietly, opening another door. It led to stairs going up to the surface world above them.

Her feet felt like weighted lead, her shoulders heavy with dread. They climbed three flights and at the emergency door, Ram moved past her and opened it for her.

Blinking, she realized they were out on street level, but not at the main entrance any longer. Weather-wise, it was sunny and beautiful. Cars were whizzing by, and everything looked so peaceful and normal. Easing out onto the sidewalk, Ram scanned the area, always on guard, always aware.

"Let's go to your apartment?" he suggested.

"Y-yes…okay…"

"Or would you rather be alone right now, Dare? I just thought you might like some company."

"I'm really feeling torn up inside, Ram…"

"I think all of us are," he rasped, giving her a patient look. "Your car is parked where?"

She pointed. "Two blocks down on the left."

"Do you want company or not?"

Nodding, she said, "It would be nice to have some private time with you. I have so many worries about this briefing…"

"You're not alone. Let's talk in private."

She heard something new in his low tone as he walked on the outside of her toward the parking lot. It was a beautiful November day, warming up, the sky a dark blue. "It's so peaceful right now…"

"Yes," he murmured. "But not for long."

"I think I need a cup of lemon balm tea. My nerves are screaming," she admitted.

"Make that two cups."

RAM FELT THE emotional storm building in Dare as she changed her clothes and reappeared in the kitchen to make them the tea in her ground-floor apartment. She wore a pair of comfortable brown trousers and a cream-colored angora sweater. How badly he wanted to slide his arms around her shoulders and bring her against him and hold her…just hold her and take away the anxiety he saw in her darkened eyes that normally shined with such life. They were dull looking right now. He wrestled inwardly with his own emotions, mostly for Adam and his family, some for his team as a whole and the rest for Dare. His protectiveness was leaking out and it seemed he didn't have the normal iron-clad control over it he used to.

"Is there anything I can do to help?" he offered, standing, his hips resting against the kitchen counter near where she was working.

"No. I got this…"

"Where do you keep the teacups?"

"Up there," and she pointed to a cabinet.

He needed to do something to help her. "I'll get them," he said.

After finding two beautiful porcelain teacups and saucers, hand-painted pink and red roses on them, he located the flatware drawer, bringing out two tea-spoons to go with them. Just the sounds of the copper teakettle being filled with water, something common and daily, was soothing to him. He saw some of her worry ease, her shoulders starting to relax. There was a modicum of peace in the rhythm of everyday life.

"Won't rose hip tea help?" he teased her gently.

She managed a one-sided partial smile. "No, it's not a nervine like lemon balm. Nervine herbs are your stress busters. They soothe the central and parasym-pathetic nervous systems."

"I see…"

"That was nice of Lera to bag you up some rose

hips so that you could have a cup a day after finding out your knees were as bad as mine."

He grinned a little, arms against his chest as he rested against the kitchen counter. She set the copper teakettle on the stove to heat. "It was. And she wouldn't take any money."

"You are family to her, Ram. The whole team is. That is how she and Adam see all of us. Any of the other guys, if they want it for their joints, all they have to do is ask and she'll supply them the rose hip powder. I think if you try it out and get good results, you should share the information with them. Lera would love to give them some. She doesn't like to see people suffer."

"As soon as I find out it works? I'll let them know." Wanting to place his hands on her shoulders as she turned to face him because she was in desperate need of being held, he reminded himself that he had said he wanted her as a friend. Not her lover. "You don't like to see people suffer either, Dare."

"You're right about that. Let's go to the living room, Ram. I'll bring the tea in on a tray and we'll sit on the couch. That okay?"

"Yes, I'd like that." His heart lifted with hope. That word *hope* had been burned out of him at eighteen, but here it was, back again. Ram didn't try to fight or suppress it this time. Instead, he ambled into her living room, the western sun flowing brightly through floor-to-ceiling windows, like a golden waterfall, into the area. Everything about her apartment was neat, clean and welcoming. She liked the color purple, he discov-

ered, the curtains across the huge picture windows fil-
tering the sunlight through light lavender ones. There
was a vase of fresh flowers that he'd given her on Sunday, before she left the Voronas' home. He smiled to
himself when he saw Dare had mixed into it a few
sprigs of rose hips on their twigs, with some bright
red maple leaves to top it off.

She came in a few minutes later with a small teak
tray bearing the teapot, cups and spoons, plus a jar
of honey that Lera had also gifted her with. The
ties between Adam's family and her were strong and
good. Ram was glad she had a "second family" here
in Kyiv because he'd discovered how much she loved
her adopted parents, who were safe in the United
States. She was a family person. He had been, too,
at one time, but that was lost to the sands of time.
His life stopped at eighteen. And he'd had to start
all over.

Looking back on it, Ram was amazed at that immature age how well he had done despite the trau-
matic life blow. He could have done a lot of things,
turned to addiction to escape his horrifying family
history, become a drunkard or done something reckless like take revenge. Having done none of those
things, and thanks to the Army he'd joined earlier,
they'd helped him through that terrible gauntlet of
shock and loss. So, he had himself to thank that he
listened and trusted the right people at that seminal
moment in his life.

Now? As Dare sat down after placing the tea service on the glass and wood coffee table in front of

them, they were all going to be at a similar moment come mid-February of next year. Everyone's life would change drastically for the worse, not the better.

He watched her pour the light-colored brown liquid. It smelled good, a sweet scent and maybe a bit of mint in it? He wasn't sure as he took a dollop of honey. Stirring it, he sat back, a good two feet separating them. He was happy that she'd sat fairly close to him. Did Dare know she needed to be held? Ram wasn't sure because she was such a strong, confident and independent woman. He admired that in her, but then, Ukrainian people had a long history in this part of the world, the ancient people being strong and resilient, too.

She sipped the tea, slowly leaning back on the flowery fabric of the couch. "Mmm, this tastes so good. Try yours?"

He nodded. The delicate porcelain cup and saucer made him feel awkward. His hands were large, square and covered with thick calluses from years of black ops duty. Compared with her hands, her skin soft and fairly unmarred, his were the opposite: white scars here and there along with pink ones, hands deeply tanned, and they weren't pretty looking at all. Sipping the tea, he made a sound in his throat.

"This tastes good, Dare."

"Lemon balm goes down easy. We need to drink the entire cup and then we'll see how we feel after that."

"Anything to come off the cliff we were just pushed over," he growled, nodding, sipping more.

She gave him a warm look, her voice off-key.

"Thanks for being here. I don't know how you knew, Ram, but I needed someone…you…"

Those were the sweetest words he never thought he'd hear Dare say.

Chapter Five

Dare poured herself a second steaming cup of lemon balm. She'd seen the surprise flicker momentarily in Ram's gray eyes when she admitted her need of him, his company. His shoulders relaxed and his eyes darkened a little as he studied her. She wasn't sure what that meant.

"I'll be the first to admit that I've never been friends with a woman, so I'm feeling like I'm skating on thin ice, here, with you."

"You have male friends, right?"

"Yes."

"Then regard me like that?"

He managed a slight grimace. "I had many friends who were boys, growing up. Girls were strange to me and I was honestly shooed away from them because I thought they acted and thought differently than boys did."

"Variety is the spice of life, Ram. If we do think and see things differently, that's not a weakness as far as I'm concerned, it's a strength. Instead, I see it as two points of view to be considered is all."

"I think men like to categorize and organize everything into neat little boxes. Nothing complex."

She gave an abrupt laugh. "Women don't fit within those so-called boxes and never will."

"Through the years you were with us, the way you thought and saw things always kept us safer."

Nodding, she sipped her tea. "I can see overall patterns, and we have the ability to zero in on the exact detail that needs to be further studied within that pattern."

"I remember you fixated on a bunch of six-foot-tall bushes near the summit of a hill we were approaching. You saw movement when none of us men did. It saved our lives. It was a trap and the Taliban was setting up to kill all of us."

Nodding, she said, "And that brings me to what's bothering me so much, Ram."

"I felt you freeze behind me at the meeting."

"Yes." She sighed. "Adam's village highway is marked as one of two main routes that the Russian tanks are going to use to destroy Kyiv."

Grimly, he nodded. "Yes... That's not good."

"We need to talk with him and Lera. They need to move out of there, Ram. They can't stay there."

"I was thinking along the same lines." He gave her a reverent look. "I figured you would be considering such an option, too."

She set the emptied cup on the coffee table. "They *have* to move, Ram. And soon. That's all there is to it. They can't stay there. I wish... I wish we could warn the whole village."

"They will be warned by village government officials," he reassured her. "What I worry about is that many of the villagers have nowhere else to go or they may not have the money to make such a move." He frowned. "There's no easy fix on this, especially since it is on such short notice and it is winter."

"I know," she grumbled, scowling. "If they stay... I don't even want to think about it." Turning to him, she set the teacup on the coffee table, hands clasped tight in her lap. "I'm racking my brain trying to figure a way to get them to leave, at least until the war is over. If Lera and the girls could go across the border, into Poland, and stay there—"

"She's tied to Ukraine, Dare. She won't leave this country. They have no relatives in Poland, either."

Pursing her lips, she closed her eyes for a moment and then opened them. "I have plan B."

His shoulders relaxed a little. "Tell me about it."

"I want to try and get them to move into central Kyiv. There's a family apartment right across the hall from me that is up for lease right now. It is large, and they would be so much safer here. I don't believe our troops will allow Russians into Kyiv. I just don't."

"We're in agreement," he said quietly. "So? There's an apartment next door and Lera and her girls could stay there?"

"Yes, and since I'll be with your team, she can also come over with the code card I'll give her, to get whatever she needs from my apartment." She gave him a swift look. "I want them out of Bucha, Ram. I don't care if Lera hates me for forcing this change on her. I'll take her anger or whatever she wants to throw at me if only she'll agree to leave the village for now."

Rubbing his jaw, he sat back on the couch after setting his cup on the coffee table. "Lera is a levelheaded person. She won't take it out on you."

"I feel you're probably right. Adam, I'm sure, will want her and the girls to leave, too. I believe he will agree with our plan and support it."

Nodding thoughtfully, he said, "It would be best for all of them. Adam will go wild with terror if the Russians capture Bucha. He knows only too well what will happen. I need him focused on our team, on our orders and mission. He won't be any good to me, otherwise."

"I hadn't even thought that far ahead," she whispered, wiping her eyes.

He studied her as the silence cloaked them. "Why tears?" he rasped gently, reaching out, placing his hand over hers momentarily. He squeezed her fingers and they were icy cold. Her fingers curled around his in response. "Dare? You can talk to me. We're going to be friends, right? Don't friends tell each other everything?"

"I—I guess I should," she managed, her voice raspy. The expression on his face was one of caring, something she'd rarely seen. His fingers gently squeezed hers, and fresh tears came to her eyes. She never cried in front of the team. Not ever. Sniffing, she wiped the tears away with her other hand.

He released her fingers and dug into his pocket, producing a white cotton handkerchief. "Here," he said, his voice low, slipping it into her hand, "use this…"

His unexpected compassion broke her. It happened without warning and Dare didn't realize until just then how much anxiety and worry for Adam's family she was carrying. Pressing the cloth to her eyes, she muttered, "I've never cried in front of you."

"I know," he answered, sadness in his tone. "You always went off by yourself, out of sight and earshot, to do it." He reached out, gently massaging her slumped shoulder. "You don't know how many times I wanted to go find you, and be supportive of you, Dare."

Wiping her eyes, she blew her nose, giving him a startled look. "You did?" she croaked.

He nodded, leaving his hand on her shoulder. "It pains me to see you suffering like that. All I wanted to do, I guess, was to hold you, console you, give you my shoulder so you had something to cry on."

Shaken, she clenched the handkerchief between her hands. "I never knew," she whispered brokenly, searching his eyes.

"I was torn about my action, my decision, Dare. My heart wanted to go after you, wanting you to cry on my shoulder, while I held you. I knew how much you were hurting. You're a medic. Medics are all heart. I desperately wanted to be with you, just to give you someone to talk with if you wanted," and he said, patting his shoulder, "to lay your head on me and cry it out." He managed a slight grimace. "I've been holding on to this secret for years. We're more mature now, Dare, and seasoned operators. We know war. It always hurt me to see you walk off, having no one there to hear your cry, or wipe your tears away, to listen to whatever you wanted to share with me…"

The silence fell softly between them. Their gazes

met and held. Dare sniffed, her face hot from the tears. "W-why didn't you tell me this before now?" Her voice was wobbly as she was unsure about what she saw, stormy emotions in his eyes, in the way he grimaced and winced when she asked the question.

"Because I was a coward, Dare. That's why."

She straightened, as if slapped, staring at him. "What? No!" The words had come out with fierceness. "You've put yourself on the line so many times for our team. I was afraid for you. You were so brave, as if you knew you were protected by some higher force for good."

"Listen to me," he rasped, choking out the words, "I was a coward for never telling you how much I wanted to care for you. I constantly fought my desire to have a relationship with you, Dare. That was the other war I was fighting within myself."

Gasping, she blinked, her lips, wet with tears, parting. "W-what?"

He dragged in a long breath of air and then released it. "There's too much at stake right now," he said, more to himself than her, his brows scrunching. He held her shocked look and added roughly, emotion nearly overwhelming him, "Dare, somewhere along the way after you joined our team in Afghanistan, I fell deeply and completely for you. I'd seen you with the sick babies in those villages, I saw you treat the women and the aged ones… I've been with you on the battlefield when Artur was gravely wounded and you saved his life…" He shook his head, giving her a look of apology.

"I was a coward for not coming clean with you, not telling you the truth. I was afraid you'd get angry, but what scared me more than anything was that you didn't have the same feelings for me. I sensed it, but neither one of us acted upon it.

"With Russia on our doorstep right now, I made a decision after the briefing today to tell you the truth because it was eating me up alive. I needed to hear how you feel. I don't want to go into battle without knowing if there might be a future for us or if there isn't. And if there isn't? You'll still be our medic and we'll work as a team. I won't hold anything against you if you don't feel reciprocal. Only you and I will know the truth between us and it is ours to keep secret with one another. The team will not know anything. We'll work together, as we always have."

Her heart was pounding furiously and she swallowed hard several times, her tears turning off by the shock of his honesty. Pushing some short strands away from her brow, she sat there digesting everything. She saw the utter suffering in Ram's face, the apology in his eyes and fear that she was going to reject him, reject his love for her.

"You couldn't let me know," she offered quietly, her voice barely above a ragged whisper. "Army regulations. And if that didn't stop you, then what did is your concern for the cohesiveness of our team. Our ability to trust one another with our lives was primary and most important. Am I right, Ram?"

Sighing, he nodded. "Yes, I couldn't see any other

way to address my dilemma, Dare. But how do you feel? That's what I need to know."

"I didn't have those feelings...at first."

Nodding, he said, "I understand."

"But something changed between us, Ram. I felt it about three months into our team being together."

"You knew then?"

"I knew something, but I had no idea what it really meant. You were like ice, Ram. No emotion when we were out on the line."

"It kept you alive, didn't it?"

She managed a snort. "Yes, it did. But you were always distant toward me. I could never figure out why. You were warm, smiling, joking and laughing with the men, but you avoided me like I was the bubonic plague."

"I was afraid I couldn't handle my escaping emotions that I held secretly for you, Dare. It wasn't you. I was *my* problem with myself. I'd had my share of relationships, but when you came into my team, you stunned me. I was never the same after meeting you."

She blew out a long breath, giving him a sideward glance. "Well, you treated me like I was off-limits as a human being, never mind someone that you were drawn to. I figured you really didn't want me in your team."

"What?" He sat up, staring in disbelief at her. "Is *that* what you thought?"

"Sure," she snapped, defensive over his sudden, raw emotional disclosure. "Look back on that time, Ram. You ignored me. You never smiled at me. You never joked with me. It was like I was some kind of virulent infection in your team. I could feel this ice coming off you toward me."

Wearily, he shook his head. "Because I wasn't mature enough, Dare. I didn't have what it took to find common ground with you, to help you know that you were wanted. I didn't know how to handle the situation, so I made sure that you would always approach me as the professional you were."

"You were afraid of yourself?"

"Yes." He pushed his fingers through his dark hair in an aggravated motion. "It's different now, of course. I've grown since then. Before, I saw you as beautiful, all heart, a warm smile…" He hesitated. "The way you smile makes my heart open up with such a rush of joy that I have no words for it. I saw you bestow that wonderful smile of yours on the Afghan babies, the children and the elderly. And you were like that with everyone on the team, too. My men loved you like a sister."

"They took me under their wing, Ram. All of them. I felt wanted and they respected me for the skills I was bringing to them in the team."

He managed a grimace and gave her a wry look. "You never piss off the medic on your team. He or she is your best friend who can save your sorry ass and get you back home to your family if you are wounded."

She shook her head. "Medics, in general, are held in esteem by everyone. No medic would refuse to save a team member's life even if they didn't like one another. They aren't built that way."

Silence grew between them. She cast a look in his direction, the suffering clearly in his expression now. "After Artur was carried aboard that Blackhawk helicopter, the paramedic on board and I worked together to keep him stable."

"I'll never forget that day," he rasped wearily. "We all sat on the deck, that helo shaking and shuddering, the noise so high we couldn't hear ourselves think. You two were working all the time on that one-hour flight back to camp. I remember thinking that you looked like an angel among us, your hands were so slender, so graceful, and that each time you touched Artur, who was unconscious on the deck, you were giving him lifesaving energy you held in your heart for him, to keep him alive."

She inhaled deeply. "My whole existence was focused on him and nothing else."

Silence again fell over them.

Ram cleared his throat. "After Artur was taken to the hospital at the camp, you were standing there alone, and we were all whipped, defeated, fearing we'd lost him and that only you had stood between him and his death. We all knew that." He reached out, gripping her hand resting on her thigh, holding her glistening gaze. "I couldn't help myself at that moment. Something old and hard snapped within me and I remember throwing my arms around your shoulders and hauling you against me. I thanked you for saving Artur's life. I lived in a hellish fear of losing anyone on my team. All I wanted to do was to get all of you safely home, out of that sandbox hell, so that you could once more see your family, and the people who loved you.

"I remember that night so clearly, Dare. I'll never forget it as long as I live. We stood there on the helicopter apron, holding on to one another. That was a healing moment for me because I knew I could have lost you that day when you ran into that crossfire and dived for where Artur lay unconscious, dragging him back, one-handed, behind a huge boulder to safety. You tore open your medical knapsack and went to work on him. Bullets were flying all around you. You saved him that day." His voice lowered. "I cared for you so much in that hour of terror. Your focus, that fierce look on your face as you worked over him… Nothing else mattered to you in that moment. You were so brave…so competent… Since then, I've always seen you as an earth angel who walks among us poor human beings, your touch bringing us life, bringing us hope."

Shaking her head, she muttered, "I don't want to burst your bubble or how you see me, Ram, but trust me, I'm no angel. Not even close…"

He cracked a poor semblance of a smile, filled with pain and memories. "It is the moment of crisis, of life and death, when you find out who you really are, and who the other person is. That day, you were like Michael the Archangel and Gabriel, all wrapped into one. You were intense, you willed your life force back into him. I saw it. The whole team did. Artur should have died, but he didn't. It was you, Dare…you…"

She scrubbed her eyes with her palms. Her heart

hurt, but it thudded with joy. "Okay," she whispered unsteadily, "it's time for me to tell you how much of a coward I am, too."

He sat up, blinking as if not hearing her accurately. "What? What are you talking about?"

"You." She raised her gaze to the ceiling and then she slanted her gaze back to him. "I was just as much of an emotional coward as you think you are, Ram."

"Tell me more?"

"You and me. Us." Sitting up, she perched on the edge of the couch and faced him fully. "What you didn't know is that I was drawn personally to you. Don't ask me how it happened, but it did. Maybe it was that day that the team came with me into the Afghan village to take care of babies. I don't know... But when I saw you holding a crying baby in your arms, I saw that icy mask of yours you always wore melt away, and I saw the real you for the first time. It blew me away, Ram. It was then I realized you weren't a robot without a heart...that you were a living, compassionate man and I came to realize what you wanted for your team, was for us to survive this duty. I got why you behaved as you did with us on a daily basis."

His lips compressed and he stared hard at her. "Wait... You were drawn to me?"

"Yes. It was that easy to admit and that hard to carry without telling you or telling anyone else. I figured your iciness was a mask you wore because you cared so much for all of us. You wanted us to live, to get home to our families...and after that realization, it was easy to allow my feelings for you to grow and take root in my heart. I couldn't speak of how I felt toward you. And I wasn't going to confide it to the team members, who were like brothers to me. I was afraid if anyone knew my secret, it could destroy the cohesiveness we had. I understand how, if we had admitted our growing attraction for one another, that it could have hurt the team as a whole and neither of us wanted that. Not ever." She reached over and gripped his hand and squeezed it. "I understood, Ram. I really did."

He cupped her hand within his large, scarred ones. "So? Where are you today? I have to know one way or another, Dare. For so many reasons…"

"When you found out I wasn't in a relationship, you almost gave yourself away to me," she whispered. "I saw the relief in your expression. I couldn't figure out that reaction."

"I almost fainted with joy when you said you weren't in a relationship," he admitted. "Not very mature of me, at all."

Nodding, she absorbed the love shining in his gray eyes for her alone. "I had lost touch with you except for those emails you'd send maybe once a month or so, of a flower you'd crossed paths with." She touched her heart. "That always gave me hope."

"Hope?"

"That someday…somehow…that we could get together just like this and really sit down and have a heart-to-heart talk with one another without the military lording over us. Just you and me. Two people…"

"Dare—" his voice dropped to a ragged whisper "—are you still drawn to me?"

She smiled a little. "Yes. Is it possible that you're still drawn to me?"

"I never stopped dreaming of you in my life. It has grown stronger and stronger with every passing year. It was eating me up alive. I needed to see you, talk to you and be honest with you..."

"Looks like it happened." She turned her hand over, sliding it into his warm, dry one. "We are in one hell of a box canyon, Ram."

His hand grew firmer around hers. "First, there is us. We've gone four years without ever saying these words, much less doing anything overt about our feelings for one another, Dare. We have a lot of things to sort out between ourselves."

"And this isn't for public consumption, Ram, not to the team, not to Lera or Adam...to no one. No one can know how we feel toward one another."

Nodding heavily, he rasped, "Externally, nothing will change. We are going into a war and we can't upset the team's cohesiveness."

"I agree," she whispered. "Besides, I need time and so do you, just to get used to the fact we want to explore what we might have."

"I was thinking the same thing," Ram agreed. "We need time to absorb all this hidden information we'd kept from one another for so long."

"Not much time left for us. We have to convince Lera and the girls to move into Kyiv."

"That's our first priority," Ram rasped. "This whole

coming month is about gearing up for that war. We have orders to be at HQ at 0900, five days a week, to continue our training as a team. So far, we still get weekends off."

"I guess, for us, this is a new kind of hell of sorts?" she suggested, trading a wry look with him.

Giving her a warm look, he said, "I'd like to get to know you, what you want, what your hopes and dreams are. You take the lead. You're fully capable of doing that."

Nodding, she said, "I do need time. We need to understand what we have, what we expect of ourselves and of one another."

He gently placed his hand over hers. "A step at a time, right?"

"The only way."

"Do you have any wine in your fridge?" he wondered, looking toward the kitchen.

"Yes. Do you want to celebrate this aha moment of ours?"

Nodding, he stood. "Don't you think it's about time?"

"Yes," and Dare stood, going to the kitchen. She had some wonderful white Ukrainian wine and poured it into two crystal glasses. Rám joined her and they stood there, touching the lip of each other's glass.

"To us," Ram said, his voice low with feeling.

"To our future, whatever it becomes," she agreed, voice barely a whisper. Dare wasn't sure what that meant right now. As she took a sip, she asked, "What if we really aren't suited for one another, Ram?"

"If it comes to that, I'll respect your decision or vice versa."

"I feel the same."

"What I want for us is that we will be grateful for what we have, respect the other, sit down and talk like adults when problems arise, and I'm sure they will. But we're mature enough, Dare, to climb those hurdles and get over them."

"We aren't really *that* old." She laughed along with him.

He took her hand, leading her back into the living room, sitting down on the couch with her. "This is a dream come true just to do this." He lifted his arm, sliding it around her shoulders, gently drawing her against him, giving her time if she didn't want that kind of closeness to speak up. And if she had resisted, he would have instantly stopped and respected that invisible but very important boundary between them.

Dare rested her cheek against his broad shoulder that carried the responsibility for the whole team, including her. "We have a lot of challenges ahead of us," she whispered. He was so close. Inhaling his scent as a man sent an awakening through her entire body. She felt a pleasant warmth begin deep within her and it sent a craving so sweet with promise, so sharp with need, that for a moment, she was carried on that primal force of him.

"I agree," he said in low tone. "There are two things going for us, Dare. First, we're mature. Secondly, we've had four years together and apart. If we can continue to hold our mutual attraction we've always had for one another, it tells me we have a chance. The bad news is, the war is coming shortly."

"And you'll have to put away your need to want to protect me, Ram. You can't do anything different. The team would know. They are a very smart, intelligent group of seasoned combat soldiers. They miss nothing."

"We'll be discreet, Dare. That I promise you. Our unspoken attraction for one another has already stood the test of four years and they aren't any the wiser."

She turned her face, rubbing her cheek against his shoulder, his scent fueling her raw, physical desire for him, regardless of the world's issues. "I remember my father telling me when I was seventeen that it's better to have loved and lost than never loved at all."

He leaned back on the couch, closing his eyes, savoring her closeness. "It's a good saying, but I don't think it fits what we have with one another. It was as if when I saw you for the first time, Dare, that I already knew you. I felt like you had walked in from the past, back into this time, to be with me once again. It was an overwhelming feeling, an intuition. No woman had ever, before you, affected me like you do."

"Star-crossed lovers, maybe?" she wondered quietly, closing her eyes, feeling the stress of the many days dissolving as she lay against him.

A rumble of a chuckle reverberated through his chest. "Crossed, for sure. But I'm a patient man and I waited."

She barely opened her eyes, thinking how many times she might get a chance to be with him just like this. It felt to her as if she were in a dream, not the cold, hard reality staring back at them presently. "I guess I'm patient, too. I had no interest in having an affair with you. It just never crossed my mind. How I feel about you, Ram, goes so much deeper than that."

"I believe it is the same for both of us."

"There was never anyone else who could stand in your shoes," she admitted.

"But now? As you Americans say? The cat is out of the bag or something like that?"

"You've been around Americans too much," she accused, laughing gently.

He sobered, holding her amused gaze, so close that he wanted to kiss her, but it was too soon…too early. She had to come to him, let him know what she did or did not want from him. The thought was warm, inviting. "I chased you until you caught me, and I will always be yours."

Chapter Six

As he sat at Adam's dining room table, comforting his sobbing wife, Lera, Ram felt as if his heart were being physically torn out of his chest. They had put the children to bed much earlier, the harsh news broken to Lera by her husband, whose face was stricken with a mix of anger toward the Russians and grief over his wife's sobs. She clung to Adam, face buried against his chest as he held her tightly. They had to leave their home and move into Kyiv for safety's sake. The look of helplessness in Adam's face as he gently smoothed his hand across her hair tore at Ram.

Glancing to his right where Dare sat, he saw she was upset and sensed she wanted to cry right along with Lera, or at least somehow comfort her as a friend. His elbows rested on the table, hands gripped tightly with the swirling energy of shock reverberating through their home. Lera had heatedly fought Adam to remain in Bucha, but in the end, it was he who had persuaded her to move near where Dare lived, and not be taken prisoner by the advancing Russian tanks that would come their way down that main highway that cut right through the middle of their village. She had capitulated because of her daughters, wanting them safe. This house was the only home she'd ever known.

Ram felt Dare's focus on him and lifted his chin, lips tightened as he met her anguished gaze. How badly he wanted to comfort her in that moment, too, just as Adam was comforting his wife. But he couldn't. Sometimes, he didn't want to be a leader of a team, and this was one of them. Asking Lera to move everything of importance to her and the children, out of their home where she and her family had lived for generations, was a big ask.

He tore his gaze from Dare and rubbed the fabric of the thick fleece shirt beneath his opened leather jacket. Nothing helped the pain he was experiencing for Adam's family.

Finally, Lera stopped crying, Dare handing her tissue after tissue from a nearby box, giving her a sad look of silent apology. Adam straightened, rubbing his face savagely, as if to rub away all that was coming their way in February.

"W-what of the other men in your team, Ram?" Lera asked, her voice stricken and hoarse with tears.

"I've talked to all of them. As you know, most of them are married. Those that aren't have extended family around central Kyiv. Few members of my team live in outlying villages around Kyiv, like this one, Lera. I'm urging all of them to either move their immediate family into Kyiv for a while, or to remain where they are unless there is a Russian attack upon them. Those who want to go to Kyiv are starting that process of moving tomorrow."

"Or," Adam rasped, giving his wife a loving look, his arm around her sagging shoulders, "Ram thinks it's best that all the families go to Poland, across the border, because Russia won't attack there since it's a NATO country. If we stay here, even in Kyiv, we will be bombarded. The only safe place for citizens will be the subway system, which is far below ground and safe for people to hide in. Already, the military is stocking food, water, medical supplies and other necessary items all along the subway routes so people have food, water and any other help they need while they are forced to stay underground for days…maybe a week or more at a time…" His voice thinned and he leaned over, kissing Lera's mussed hair as she mopped her face with another tissue.

"I won't go to Poland!" Lera cried out, banging her fist on the table, glaring at Adam and then at Ram. "I don't know anyone there! I don't speak their language!"

"You can stay in Kyiv, near Dare's apartment. I will draw out all our savings and checking from the bank," Adam told her. "You will carry the money on you or keep it in your apartment. My military salary will be electronically sent to your smartphone, Lera, not to the bank. You will always have funds to live, to purchase food and to take care of the children's needs while in Kyiv."

Ram listened to Adam's low, quiet voice soothing his fractious wife, whose expression was one of terror mixed with incredible sadness, frustration and anger. She was being asked to leave everything she ever knew behind. He had no doubt Russians would soften up the village with artillery or missile strikes. And then their tanks would roll in, so close to the jugular point where he and many other black ops teams were being ordered to stop them and halt their forward movement into Kyiv itself. The tanks would shoot to kill. They wouldn't care if there were civilians, women or children murdered.

He knew Russian atrocity up front and close, even though he'd never spoken to anyone about it. They were hardened soldiers, cruel, heartless and without any morals or values. They refused to follow Geneva Conventions. He knew they considered civilians as justified targets to shoot and kill. It made no difference to them. It was so hard for him not to speak of it, to scare Lera enough into leaving with the girls for safety, but he couldn't give Russian inhumanity a voice.

Ram kept his tone low and sincere. "We'll help you, Lera. Adam, my team and I will do the heavy lifting around the house. If you and Dare could pack boxes, suitcases or whatever else you would want for a leased apartment? That would be good." He opened his hands, seeing a sense of helplessness as her eyes once more filled with tears.

"Will they burn our house down, Ram? What will they do?"

It felt like a knife twisting in his gut. Grimly, he rasped, "It could happen, Lera. I'm sorry...so sorry.

But think if you and the children were in this house when a missile hit it? Or a tank fired a shot into it? Blowing it up? It would kill or wound all of you. I know that isn't what you want. You have to leave in order to live…"

Dare reached over, her hand gently laying over Lera's lower left arm. "We'll do this together. I'm really good at organizing. We can make a list. I've already talked to the manager at the apartment building, and he says you are welcome to lease that family-sized apartment across the hall from where I live. He's holding it open for lease to you and Adam. I hope you'll say yes. I will be out in the field with Ram and the team, and you'll have the code card for my apartment across the hall-way from yours. You can use it and anything in it you might need while I'm gone. The manager is a woman and she is very warmhearted. She's willing to help your family any way she can. You are only half a block from the entrance to the subway. You will be able to reach it if Putin starts sending missiles into Kyiv. That under-ground subway will save your lives."

Nodding, wiping her eyes, she whispered, "All right… We'll go and yes, I need all your help…"

"There's a rental company a block away from that apartment building," Ram told her, "and anything you don't want to take? We can store there, until this war is over."

Jerkily nodding, Lera sniffed, took another tissue from Dare and blew her nose. "We will go. *But…* I want us to still have the American Thanksgiving, Dare.

You talked so much about it. I wanted to make it for you, a celebration…"

Smiling a little, Dare choked out, "We'll have Thanksgiving over at the high-rise. That's only weeks away, Lera. I'll help you make it over there, okay?"

With a nod, Lera turned and looked up at her husband. "Are you all right with this?"

He kissed her hair. "I am," he rasped. "I think we can all use a US Thanksgiving at the end of November. I've never had a turkey dinner, as Dare calls it, but we'll all work to get the family and goods moved in so we can celebrate it together. It will be a happy time for all of us, especially the girls."

November 9

THE FIRE WAS LOW, mostly coals glowing, sending out sparse light into the living room. Dare sat on the rug in front of the warmth, cozy in her hooded velvet robe, which fell to her feet. It was 3:00 a.m. and she couldn't sleep, so she'd gotten up to make herself some lemon balm tea.

A noise made her sit up.

"Sorry," Ram offered quietly at the opening to the living room. "I didn't know you were out here—"

"We're making a habit of this."

He managed a slight smile. He was dressed in his dark burgundy pajamas and a dark blue robe. His feet were bare. "My mind is going a million miles an hour. I can't close my eyes and sleep it off or make it go away."

She patted the braided rug next to where she sat,

her knees drawn up against her body, arms around them. "Come sit by me. Right now, it's nice to have company."

He pushed his hair away from his brow and sat down nearby, but not so near, he hoped, as to make her pull away from him. The last week had been devoted to meetings and more briefings. He saw little of Dare except in a professional capacity. Settling down, he absorbed the low light and warmth coming from the many coals in fireplace, thinking how beautiful and courageous she looked to him. He was still reeling from their open discussion about their love for one another; almost feeling as if it were some kind of dream.

He was afraid of the approaching war. It could be a nightmare that would destroy what they'd just found with the other. The hope in his heart had blossomed. After all these years, their feelings were mutual. It was a dream enclosed by a coming nightmare.

"Do you think Lera and Adam are sleeping? Or are they tossing and turning like we did?" she wondered softly, giving him a long, warm look.

He sat cross-legged, pulling the ends of his robe across his knees and thighs. "I don't know. Adam is a great leader and he knows how to deal with thorny situations well. I believe their love for one another will see them through this chaos and change, but it doesn't hurt that Adam won't let his emotions run away with him and make reckless mistakes, either. He's clear-headed about this. I know he's relieved that Lera and the girls will be in Kyiv, even if he won't say it to her. He doesn't want to see her cry again."

"Just because some women are emotional and cry more openly doesn't mean that we make reckless mistakes. We can behave courageously when things are going terribly wrong. We choose our time to cry, Ram. Just as I suspect you, and the rest of our team, does, also."

He felt a powerful, nearly overwhelming need to coax her into his arms, to have her come and lean against him and hold her. "You're right, of course."

"Women are warriors, don't ever forget that. Sure, I can fire a weapon and I can kill just like any of you can, but that doesn't mean I'm carrying my emotional reactions into the firefight, because I don't."

"The women of Ukraine are fierce wolves at heart. They are patriotic, and their family and our country mean everything to them."

"Just like the Black Wolf badge ID we wear on our fatigues," Dare said, "we are wolves in a pack and it's our duty to protect the civilians of this country. But the women of Ukraine will fight this battle, too. Maybe not like our team does, but they will be on the front lines in so many small, everyday ways, as well."

"Exactly, but I'm afraid, Dare, that most of the people of Bucha will stay, and not leave. I know the government agencies are desperately trying to persuade them to leave now. But you know how adamant we are about our home, our family and the generations that have been in that same house or farm for a hundred years or more. It's hard for them to move under those circumstances."

"Many won't leave," Dare agreed softly, frowning.

"You are a people of the land. You are tied to it. Your roots are deep and forever, I know that. And I understand it." Shaking her head, she whispered sadly, "This is one time they need to leave..."

"There's talk of about two million of our people, mostly grandparents, wives with children, will be leaving for Poland. I was talking with our Polish diplomat today before we left after the last briefing. He said Poland is doing everything in their power to arrange help, housing, food, medicine and prepping their schools to handle Ukrainian children."

"It's a horrifying mess for everyone," she muttered fiercely, frowning. "Damn the Kremlin."

"I live to see every last one of them in hell."

"Well, we're going to get our chance to rip them a new one, Ram. We're at the point of the spear on this one. The government is counting on the black-ops-trained troops to stop the tanks in their tracks, no matter which direction they come from. They will keep Kyiv safe from this enemy tank brigade...and fight for the country as a whole. Ukraine will survive this."

He felt his heart tearing, not even wanting to think of what would happen if she was killed in combat. The helplessness that flowed through him was bitter and slicing. "Yes," he managed, "my dream is to protect the country. But I fear the worst..."

November 12

AS DARE DROVE her car into an aboveground parking lot next to her apartment building, it was well past midnight. Ram's truck was also parked nearby. "You have an hour-long drive to your house," she said, pulling in and turning off the engine and lights. They'd just finished a late-night briefing. There was another early morning meeting for Ram.

Yawning, he managed, "Nothing new..."

The streetlights of Kyiv shed shadows and brightness into her vehicle. "You know I have a spare bedroom?"

"Yes." He slanted a look in her direction and saw that gleam in her eyes. That always meant trouble, but not necessarily bad trouble. She compressed her lips and turned, her one arm hooked over the steering wheel, staring at him.

"Stay with me tonight? Don't try to make that drive home. You have to be as emotionally blasted by that last briefing as the rest of us were. You'd have an hour's drive back into Kyiv tomorrow morning to make that 0700 meeting. If you stay with me? That is two extra hours you can get some badly needed sleep."

He stilled the surprise and didn't allow it to translate to his face. "Yes, I'll take you up on your guest bedroom." He drew a long breath and said, "We used the day for moving Adam and his family and then, this unexpected call from HQ and emergency briefing tonight. Since we've started moving them into that apartment, they are protecting their daughters from a lot of the truth of why they're doing it."

"Lera is making it a fun move for them, getting them excited about a new place to live. They don't have a grasp of their generations of family history in that house or the sadness Lera and Adam feel about moving out of it. I feel so badly for all them…helpless…"

He reached out, sliding his hand that rested on her thigh. "And the girls are overjoyed that Auntie Dare is right across the hall from them. I've seen that as we moved their boxes and furniture into their apartment, that you take them into your apartment and keep them distracted. I know Lera and Adam are grateful for your help.

"We're making good progress in the move, despite all these briefings we're having to attend, to get them here in Kyiv," Ram continued. "Every day, Lera looks less upset. She does like the new apartment and it's looking almost lived in, now. I think another week, and they will be settled in and the worst will be over for them."

"I agree," she whispered, turning her hand over, lacing her fingers between his. "Until then? I want to play, take care of and be with the girls whenever I can. I know Lera is overwhelmed in getting the apartment livable, as well as cooking for her family. I'm going to continue to cook for them when I have a chance." She hesitated and said, "Look, I think we need to circle the wagons here, Ram. Tactically, from here on out, you should stay in my apartment until we are ordered to the front lines. Adam isn't going to be able to help Lera much because of his duties to the team that he's responsible for as the number two in command. If you stay with me, you're close to everything and you can give your support as you can." She tilted her head. "How do you feel about this idea?"

He rubbed his jaw and rasped, "Tactically? It works. Lera is emotionally exhausted. She'll no longer have her part-time job, either. The girls will need to be placed into new schools. There's a lot to juggle right now. I like your idea. Are you comfortable with me in the same apartment with you?"

"I trust you, Ram." Her voice lowered. "I'm hoping it will allow us a little more personal time together, time to talk with one another. There just isn't that much time left to us before the Russians are on our doorstep."

"Our trust in one another is solid," he agreed, his tone serious. "I'd like nothing better than to juggle my workload with helping Lera and Adam." He saw relief in her expression.

"I'm as emotionally torn up as you are, Ram. It would be nice if you were closer. You always steadied me out in tight situations when we were out in the field in Afghanistan."

His brows moved up. "I did?" He saw her give him a rolled-eyed look. "What?"

"I still haven't figured out whether you're symbolic of the fool's card from the tarot deck, the young man stepping off the cliff, into space, not a care in the world, faith that even though he was walking on nothing but air he will not fall to his death, or if you're clueless."

"Can I choose to take the cliff walker?" he teased gently, seeing the darkness beneath her eyes, the fatigue in her gaze. He absorbed the length of her fingers, how warm they were, and although she was strong in combat, right now she appeared comforted by his nearness. It made him feel good, love for her rising within him. Dare trusted him in the most important of ways.

She gave an abrupt laugh over his mild teasing. "You've got a bear trap mind, Ram."

"I really made you feel better out in the field?" It was hard to believe because her aura was one of sheer, rock-solid confidence. The men of his team utterly trusted her and would give their lives for her, if necessary, but she would do the same for them, too. They were like brothers with a big sister among them.

"You have no idea." Giving him a searching look, she whispered, "There's so much I want to share with you."

"But not tonight, Dare. Your game plan is solid and I'll stay here with you. Later this week, I'll drive out to my apartment and get my clothes and gear and bring them into the spare bedroom. Right now? We need to sleep. And from here on out? We're either going to be up to our neck in helping Adam's family adjust, or being ordered to more and more briefings before we receive our orders. At some point? They'll send us out in the field."

"I know…" She squeezed his hand, pulled her fingers free and climbed out of the car.

As Ram egressed from the car, as always checking the area out, he remained slightly to the right of Dare's shoulder and a step behind her. It was a protective guard position. The night was chilly, the wind blowing sporadically. All up and down the empty sidewalk, the trees grew along it, bare and naked in the harsh street-lights, making the shadows look like skinny monsters in his imagination, just waiting to ambush someone. He followed her through the outer door that opened with her card. There was a second entrance and she punched in the key code.

Once inside her apartment, he glanced around, well aware that she was heading down the hall. He followed her as she had opened up a closet and handed him two sheets and pillowcases.

"You have to make the bed. The folded blankets are at the end of it. Each room has a full bathroom." She shut the door and turned, looking up at him. "I'll see you in the morning, Ram. Good night." She stretched upward and kissed him gently on his mouth.

Caught off guard, his arms loaded with linens, the warmth of her lips against his stunned him. It was a quick kiss, and she stepped away, giving him a look that raced through his entire being. In that moment, there was such love shining in her eyes that he'd never seen before, it left him mute with surprise.

"Sleep well," he managed, watching her walk down the hall, turn left and disappear.

Progress. Yes, it was progress. She had kissed him! Out of the blue. Completely unexpected! He behaved like a teenager, in total shock. Shaking his head, he stood there in the semidarkness of the hall, alone, but inwardly celebrating their first kiss. The imprint of her full lips against his filtered through him, melting the hard walls he'd erected inside himself long ago so he didn't have to feel the eviscerating pain of loss. Miraculously, as those walls dissolved, he felt joy…real joy, for the first time since his childhood. She completed him and he knew it. He turned, walking quietly toward the spare room. Dare trusted him in her home. As tired as she was? He was even more tired. The emotional ups and downs with Adam and Lera were stressful because he was a person who instituted changes to get things done, but this was different. This wasn't a tactical or strategy situation. These were two people he loved, wrestling with the nightmare that was about to overtake their country. As would it be for all Ukrainians. It was a sobering reality and he opened the door to the second bedroom.

Still… Despite it, Dare had the courage, the need for him, to kiss him just now. How many times had he wanted to take her into his arms and kiss her? Too many times to count. Ram had always reined in his need for Dare, giving her the space she needed. Now, he knew without a doubt that his decision to allow her to lead had been correct. He felt such peace that it seemed unreal. *One kiss. Her kiss.* When she'd leaned upward, pressing her mouth to his, he inhaled her sweet scent. She loved the Hawaiian plumeria scent and tonight he'd inhaled it like life itself into his terribly broken inner world. The kiss had awakened his other emotions, good ones, that had been packed away in cold storage within himself because they had nowhere else to survive. *Until now. Right now.* She had breathed her life into him. And for the first time since he was eighteen, he felt real hope. Real love.

Standing in the large room, a queen-size bed in the middle of it, he placed the linens on the mattress and got undressed. A good hot shower was a welcome friend and first up on his agenda. Tomorrow was another day. They had it off and he would be able to help Adam and Lera get settled into their apartment. In his heart, he felt light and happy. Right now, that was all this was: a dream. Real life intruded and surrounded them. He ached to hold Dare in his arms, to feel her warm, supple body next to his. More than anything, he wanted time, quality time, with her, alone...

November 20

SNOW WAS FALLING outside the large floor-to-ceiling windows of Dare's apartment. It was late afternoon and she'd gotten some time alone. Adam and Lera's household had settled into their new apartment. She missed Ram. He'd been on a three-day undercover assignment, top secret, and he could tell no one about it. Last night, she'd dreamed once more of kissing him. What would it be like to have their lips meet again? He'd changed in subtle but wonderful ways since her bold kiss with him in the hallway. She felt achy between her thighs, wanting him in every way. Through no fault of their own, life around them was speeding up, intensifying, and so many others needed emotional support and help right now. There were families leaving Kyiv and taking the trains to Poland now by the thousands. Some were leaving the beautiful city and Dare didn't blame them. Adam and Lera's children were now in their new school, and Lera was settling in well. It was a time of quiet chaos and she ached to see Ram.

Sitting down in an upholstered rocker, her favorite because it showed Kyiv outside the massive windows that she loved so much, she yearned to have Ram here with her. Each had to attend meetings. After a mind-bending briefing earlier, her head ached and so did her emotions. Briefings were literal and gutting, no fluff, no hiding the bare truth.

Dare closed her eyes after placing her feet on a padded stool in front of the rocker. She moved it slowly back and forth. It always reminded her of a mother rocking her child. At some point, she fell asleep, the snow falling in big, fat flakes, twirling silently from the light gray sky surrounding the city.

RAM OPENED THE door to the apartment as silently as he could. It was 1800, 6:00 p.m., and he slipped inside, quietly shutting the door. Near the front of the windows, Dare had fallen asleep in her favorite rocker. He smiled a little, walking in a way that he couldn't be heard across the oak floor that shined a deep blond color even in the winter twilight. Dare was still in her camo uniform, her polished black boots resting on the stool cushions, her hands in her lap, head tipped back, revealing the beauty of her slender throat. There were still slight shadows beneath her eyes and he knew why. The drumbeat of war coming closer every day, putting a daily stressor on her and his team.

After placing everything he carried on the kitchen

table, he shucked out of his camo coat and dark green knit cap and placed them quietly over a chair. The night would be short-lived for him, another 0700 briefing tomorrow morning. It felt so good to be alone with her, to finally get a chance to be with her, talk with her, listen to her and continue to discover and mend their past with one another. More than anything, he wanted to share a second kiss with her, this time initiated by him. Since the first one, he'd had nothing but wonderful, happy dreams at night, which was completely unlike him. He knew it was because of Dare. She completed him.

Above all, he knew how tired she was and he left everything in the kitchen, went to her bedroom and found a spare blanket. Being careful, he placed it over her, absorbing the light moving across her thick lashes against her cheeks, the softness of her skin, the way it curved, showing the strength of who she was. Forcing himself to leave, he quietly retrieved a sandwich from the refrigerator and remained in the living room, near her.

There was something peaceful about Dare that he couldn't put his finger on. It was a feeling, not an idea or thought. Frowning, he sat there after eating, his elbows on his open thighs, staring off into the darkness of the cold, snowy night. There were few people on the sidewalks now, the lamplight glowing pale yellow to a deep gold, creating dark and interesting shadows along the broad sidewalks on either side of the six lanes of highway.

He got up, washing his hands in the sink, careful to

keep the noise down, wiping them on a nearby hand towel. Dare had to attend a daylong medical combat briefing in another part of the same building where he and Adam were also located, getting another kind but equally important report. Moving quietly back into the living room, the warmth making him take off his green sweater, which he hung over one arm of the sofa, he sat down, simply absorbing Dare sleeping.

He closed his own eyes and promptly fell asleep, peacefulness stealing into every part of his being because, for the first time in his life, he was with the woman he'd so deeply fallen for so long ago. Even better? There was mutual attraction between them that was genuine. His last thoughts were that the world might be spinning out of control, but the soft impression of Dare's lips pressed to his in that surprise goodnight kiss dissolved all his worry and anxiety. For tonight? Everything was right in his world.

Chapter Seven

November 21

Ram was the first to enter Dare's empty apartment. It was near 1600 and he knew she had a meeting with the medical corps and wouldn't be home until 1700, according to their schedules for the day. He'd gone across the hall, checked in on Adam and his family. They were settling in fine. Let this time, he thought, be special for the family. Soon enough, his team would be out in the freezing weather once the Russians attacked their country.

He'd brought precooked meals home with him, setting them out on the kitchen counter, wanting to prepare them a hearty meal. Knowing Dare would be tired when she got home, he had no contact with her all day due to their separate military demands upon them. He wondered if Dare felt as starved for him as he was for her, wanting to close that four-year gap that had kept them away from one another. He placed the foil-wrapped dinners into the oven at a low temperature, put the lush salad in the refrigerator, found a couple of crystal wineglasses and opened an expensive bottle of burgundy wine to let it sit and air. Glancing at his watch, he saw it was 1715. Soon, Dare would be home.

Home. The word struck him so deeply, as it always did. Tonight he needed to come clean with her, as never before. She had to know the rest of his story, why he was the way he was. More than anything, he knew Dare's huge, compassionate heart would understand why he was so closed up, why he never talked about his family, his parents or their wheat farm. Ram would time it. He didn't want it to be a wet blanket and ruin their evening meal together. Dare was just as starved as he was to be together. She didn't need his explanation, but it was a driving fist in his heart to tell her the whole truth of who he was.

He heard the front door to the apartment open and walked toward it. Dare was in her winter uniform, gray, white and black camos. She set her briefcase inside the door and shut it.

"Hey," she said, smiling, "I smell something good."

He approached her, opening his arms, and drowned in the glistening love shining in her eyes for him alone. "Dinner is warming up in the oven," he told her, pulling her tightly against him, her arms going around his shoulders, her entire body pressed hungrily against his. Dare left no question about what she wanted from him, kissing him deeply and then pulling away, looking up at him, smiling.

"I think you want dessert first?"

He grinned. "Do you?"

She pouted. "No, I'm starving, Ram. I missed lunch today."

He eased her out of his arms and said, "Go get changed. I'll set the table for us." Nothing felt so good as to give her small gifts of love in so many different ways as he saw her entire expression soften.

"That sounds so good," she whispered, kissing his cheek and releasing his hand. "I'm going to get a quick shower and then I'll be ready to eat."

"Go," he said, giving her rear a gentle pat. "Take care of yourself, first." Because he knew Dare all too well on this one. How many times, when out at an Afghan village, she would work tirelessly from dawn to dusk, even into the night, with one of the team members holding a flashlight in a hut, to care for a sick infant or woman, and he had to order her to come back to the camp. She was always deeply touched by the health needs of the children, mothers and the elderly, wanting to help them and relieve their suffering.

Turning, he went back to the kitchen. Ram's heart soared with such incredible happiness he could barely think. That was how Dare affected him, but now, he could allow those sweeping emotional feelings to tunnel through him with rapture and joy instead of suppressing them. She was his. She loved him and he loved her.

"Mmm," Dare hummed softly, leaning over, kissing Ram's cheek, "that was a delicious meal and dessert." She saw the color of his eyes change and that was something she noticed last night when they'd lingered and kissed. And kissed again and again…until she wanted more. It was then they wisely stepped away from one another, knowing sleep was so important, that they had a long day ahead of them. His eyes had turned an antique gold color again. They sat on the sofa, him in the corner, his arm around her shoulders as she leaned against him. How thirsty she was for his closeness, the gentleness that existed within him. She'd seen a remarkable difference, a good one, and it made her whisper, "Why are you so different now?"

He tipped his head, meeting her question. "I'm not different. Am I?"

She sat up, her knee against his thigh. "I've never seen this side to you before, Ram. I like it…love it, actually. It's a wonderful surprise. Are you like this when you aren't responsible for the team?"

Frowning, he moved his palm gently up and down her thigh next to his. "Probably." He took a deep breath, released it and said, "There's something else I need to share with you, Dare. I couldn't talk about it until just now." He shook his head. "It's about me, my past… It haunts me and you need to know about it because it affects my life whether I want it to or not. I don't want you walking into a serious relationship with me and not know who I am, warts and all."

Her smile subsided and she heard and felt a heaviness in his voice, his eyes growing dark as he looked away for a moment. Whatever it was, it was serious.

"I know we haven't had time, space or place to know about all our warts," she offered, hoping to lift some of the darkness she felt cloaking him. "You know about my past. And you're right—when you're adopted as I was, it always leaves questions that probably will never be answered. It will affect me for the rest of my life. I try not to allow it to swallow me. I look at how fortunate I was to be adopted, instead. To be loved…"

"You had a lot of courage telling me about your past," he said, turning and gently brushing her cheek. "Now? I need to tell you about mine. It's time. There is no good way to tell it, but I want it out in the open between us so that you understand the private, inner hell I live with. There are nights when I can't sleep because of it. I still have nightmares and flashbacks, Dare. I don't want to scare you if I have one again."

She frowned. "Like PTSD kind of flashbacks or nightmares? We all get those. You know that. We can't be in a war situation and not be wounded by it one way or another. The entire team has them. It's just part and parcel of what happens to us in combat."

He gripped her hand that rested on his knee. "No argument about that, and no, it's a different kind of war that happened to me and that's what I need to share with you." He saw the worry in her expression, her fingers feeling warm and comforting to him as he allowed all of that grief, rage and darkness to flow unchecked through him.

"Have you told anyone else about it?"

Shaking his head, he gave her a rueful look. "I couldn't, Dare. It scares me to go back to that time, what I saw, what I lost. And I'm never sure if I can control my emotions. So far, I have…"

"Then you should share it with me. You have been in my heart since I met you. I truly believe love is the greatest healer on the face of our Earth. And whatever it is? We can handle it together."

He managed a partial smile. "You convinced me a long time ago that women are far stronger, more resilient in times of life-and-death stress than we men are. We're brittle in comparison. I've seen you in every imaginable stress situation and it's as if you are able to absorb the moment and still keep your full focus on what's going on. I've always respected and admired that about you." Giving her what he hoped was a look of love despite the roiling storm gathering more intensely within him, he said, "Let me start from the beginning. When I'm done, you ask me your questions, Dare. Okay?"

"Okay," she whispered, "I won't interrupt." She adjusted how she sat and took his hand in hers, resting it on her thigh, facing him.

Drawing in a ragged breath, he began, his voice low and unsteady. "I was born in the Donetsk Province, in Crimea of Ukraine. In 2014, Russia stole Crimea away from Ukraine. They were sending in special units of Spetsnaz troops into that region, for decades, long before Putin attacked in 2014." His hand grew sweaty and he released hers, wiping it on his other thigh to get rid of the perspiration. Looking up, he saw how concerned she was over his reaction to his story thus far but said nothing.

"Four generations of my family had a large wheat farm on that land. I grew up with members of my extended family, my grandparents, aunts, uncles and many cousins. There were ten homes in the central area of our large farm, plus my brothers, Symon and Vasyl, who were two years younger than me. We were like a small village with our family. I had told my father that I wanted to be in Ukraine's Black Wolf regiment, in black ops, and not be a farmer. He was, of course, discouraged by my choice, but Vasyl eagerly stepped up and told him he would stay at the farm and run it after my mother and father wanted to retire. I was relieved and grateful to Vasyl for his choice." Shrugging, he muttered, "I guess I was like Marco Polo. I wanted to see the world, I wanted to fight for Ukraine's freedom. So at eighteen, I left the farm and went into Army boot camp. Of course, I stayed in close touch with all my family. I missed them, I missed their love, their laughter, the good times we always had together. Everyone worked on the farm, we had five hundred hectares, or roughly twelve hundred acres of wheat that we grew every year, and it took everyone to harvest it, bring it to the nearby village's granary and then have it trucked to the coast to be put on tanker ships that would go around world, delivering it to other countries.

"I was training for the Black Wolf regiment," he began heavily, his brow deeply wrinkled, "when I received an unexpected call from my commanding officer. I hurried over to the main office area and—" his voice lowered to a bare whisper, edged with grief "—and he told me that Russia had suddenly attacked Crimea, to take it away from the Ukraine. He told me that my family's farm had been attacked by Russian

Spetsnaz troops. That they had murdered everyone, and then burned nine of the ten houses to the ground."

Gasping, Dare pressed her hand to her mouth to stop from crying out. Her eyes widened as she considered what he'd just said.

As he rubbed his face wearily, Ram's voice grew hard. "They flew me to Donbas, and I arrived with a Black Wolf team because they weren't sure where the Russians might still be in that area. They had moved on, so we were able to land the military helicopter to see it for ourselves...to see if there were any survivors. I couldn't believe my eyes. There were so many ambulances there, body bags...my God, so many body bags laying out to be taken to Kyiv and the morgue... all of my family. Their homes were destroyed. The farm's mechanic's shed remained and the Russians didn't touch the equipment or the barns with the animals in them. We'd seen this happen before in the Donbas, years earlier. The Russians would sneak in and would kill everyone who lived on that parcel of land, and then set up a Russian puppet owner to take over everything, the land, the wheat...everything. They did the same thing with my family. They murdered every one. I saw the blood on the ground here and there, the houses charred skeletons, still smoking from the fires."

Dare moved forward, sliding her arms around his broken, slumped shoulders, the look of bleakness and the soul-deep grief etched in his expression. She wanted to hold him. He roughly murmured her name, slid his arms around her shoulders, drawing her hard against him, burying his face against her neck. He was trembling. And she could feel how hard he was struggling not to allow his emotions to overwhelm him. Intuitively, she realized Ram needed to cry, to finally relieve himself once and for all of the toxic, lethal shock he'd carried alone for so long. She held him and wondered if he'd ever cried over the loss of his beloved family and extended family.

There were no words she could say to him to make him feel better. The adopted part of her, the part of her abandoned by her real mother, understood all too clearly what it meant not to have family. Ram's situation was so much worse than hers. No wonder he had been bottled up and unavailable in a human sense with his team. He'd been all business, his only priority to keep his team together and come through the war alive and able to go home to their families. Now, she knew why it was his priority, the reason behind it.

Hot tears spilled down her cheeks and Dare didn't care if Ram wanted to see them or not. What a terrible loss he'd endured for so long, by himself. Was that why he was never seen with a woman? Adam had sometimes spoken to her about his loner lifestyle, worried about Ram because he couldn't figure out why he didn't have a relationship with someone, get married, have children and raise a family. Yet, as their leader, he'd always been fair with his team, never raising his voice, but that deadly calm of his that kept everyone in control of their own emotions was always there, embracing and steadying them. Sometimes, she'd thought he was a robot without a heart, but how wrong she'd been! Dare would never tell him that. He was hurt and scarred for life, to the core by the loss of his entire family. Ram was the keeper of intense, deep and dark secrets. What internal strength he had to be able to tightly control them, not allow them into the light of day or to affect his performance as a leader.

She'd promised not to speak until he was finished and now it was so hard not to say something to him. He held her so tightly that she could barely take in half a breath of air into her lungs, the feeling around him as if he were going to explode into a million grieving pieces. How could he have gone so long without unburdening himself? That defied description in her world. She became aware of her shoulder feeling damp where he'd buried his head, and it finally dawned upon her that he was silently crying. It was the best thing in the world for him; a release of so many years of grief held internally and never given voice. Until now. With her.

She pressed a kiss to his hair, and with her other hand, she began to slowly move her palm across his tight, tense shoulders, trying to soothe away some of his pain and loss he carried so long. Her heart bled for him. He'd been all alone in the world in ways she'd never had to deal with. No more birthdays to celebrate, never another child welcomed into the family's world, or to become an uncle, or never to be able to speak with his brother, Vasyl, or take part in wonderful yearly family ceremonies. Most of all, she wanted to cry over the loss of his parents... More tears fell and she clung to him as tightly as he did to her. Grief laid a person open and it was devoid of safety. The person was at their most vulnerable and unable to protect or defend themselves from the wound. If only she could somehow…somehow ease that terrible loneliness and heavy burden he carried.

WHAT TIME WAS IT? Ram was entrapped in grief, confused and unsure of where he was. He vaguely remembered sobbing until it felt like his guts were being torn out of him. And through it all, Dare had held him, her touch healing as she moved her hand across his drawn-up shoulders and slowly up and down his back. With every pass of her hand upon him, a little more of his grief dissolved and he felt more relief, a lessening of the weight he'd carried as a result. She was magical. He'd always known that about her, and now, he was on the reciprocating end of it, just like the children and elderly Afghans who stood patiently in line for an hour or more just to be seen by her. The gentleness of Dare's calming voice, her meeting the person or child's fearful gaze, very gently touching them in a loving, caring way, and watching their face glow with hope, and watching the fear dissolving in its wake… Dare gave everyone hope and optimism in this toxic, dangerous world they all lived within.

Slowly, his groggy, clouded mind realized he was lying across half the couch. Dare was sleeping against him, her arm wrapped around his torso and cheek resting on his shoulder. He knew they were both beyond fatigue and this proved it. Wanting his head to clear more, he concentrated on her slow breathing, how good it felt to him to have her arm around him, as if to hold him safe during the storm of his grueling release. Looking up, he could see the clock on the fireplace mantel, and that it was well past midnight.

The weight of his grief made him raw as never before. What would Dare think of him now that he'd sobbed openly, without pause, and couldn't control what had been eating him alive internally for so long? Yet, just the way her arm curved around him produced solace and comfort. Miraculously, he felt lighter, not heavier. He had hatred and rage toward Russians that inhabited him from the day his family had been murdered. It had lessened enormously.

Could one person do this much for another person? Lift him out of the cauldron and not feel it eating away at his soul as it always did? He lay there, couch pillows against his back, supporting both of them, looking up at the shadowy ceiling, feeling the shock that something transformative had occurred deep within him. Something healing. He inhaled the scent of her hair, and it was like smelling a fragrant flower, drawing it deep into his lungs, feeling the scent move within him, healing him, too, in another unexpected way.

It was love, he finally realized. How much Dare loved him. It was beyond him to understand all that had just transpired. There was no science to measure the openness of a kind heart like Dare's, but look at the result. He felt so much cleaner within himself that it shocked him all over again as he absorbed the weight of her body curved against his own. They fit so well together, complementing and supporting one another. Closing his eyes, his arms around her, he felt like a starving thief for stealing her warmth, her care, the faint moisture of each breath she took against his neck. *Life.* She was life. She was *his life.* A powerful emotion, startling and yet fierce, flowed through his entire being like a tsunami. This time, it purified, freeing him in ways he wouldn't have ever imagined possible. It was as if his tears had transformed him from a dead man walking into a newly born human being with raw pulsing hope through him, an incredible rainbow of feelings that were gently and quietly swirling throughout him, washing him free of so much of the darkness he had carried.

Closing his eyes, he held her as she slept. Imprinting this night, this moment into his mind and his opening heart, he drifted off to sleep again. Only this time, it was a sleep of peace and dreams, good dreams of a future with her.

November 22

IT WAS NEAR 0600 when Dare slowly awoke. She found herself in her bed, still dressed but covered with a warm blanket. She heard the door open and forced herself to sit up. Blinking, trying to wipe the grogginess away, she noticed Ram standing in the doorway, looking properly apologetic with two cups of coffee in hand. He had changed and she could see that he'd taken a shower and shaved.

"I must have really been tired last night," she said as she sat up, bringing her legs over the edge of the mattress, reaching for the cup he offered her.

Ram went to sit in a rocker nearby. "It was a rough night for both of us. How are you feeling this morning?"

She sipped the hot brew and looked over the cup at him. "Barely awake...and you're right, last night was hard on you. I should ask how *you* are doing."

He sat back, holding her drowsy blue gaze. "Much better. I felt like some kind of magical miracle happened to me last night, thanks to you, thanks to your care."

She smiled a little. "Because you finally gave up your terrible secret and the awful grief you carried for so long by yourself, Ram. It always helps to talk it out with someone else, to dispel it. Is this the first time you've told anyone about what happened?"

Nodding, he rasped, "You're the only one, Dare. I've never cried over their loss, either. Before, I was filled with revenge, hatred and rage. I had no room left for tears."

She closed her eyes for a moment. "I don't know how you were able to hold all that inside you for so long without breaking."

"Hate is a powerful emotion, Dare. I don't urge anyone to carry it around like I've been doing. All I wanted to do was get back at the Russians for taking generations of my family away from me, the land, their homes... And I will wreak my vengeance on them. That is coming."

Sipping the coffee, she whispered, "No one can blame you for how you feel. I don't."

"But you're right—holding it in has hurt me," he offered, shaking his head. "Last night, I realized that I carried all that hatred within me for so many years."

"I can compare my adoption experience along a similar line," she whispered, pushing fingers through her unruly hair, moving a strand behind her ear. "For so long, I hated my unknown mother. I hated her because she threw me away. I realized when I was older that my rage and anger toward her was misguided. My adopted mother worked with me on that issue. I was eighteen when I finally released my hate toward her and instead started seeing her as a confused, scared, immature young woman who didn't know what else to do with an unwanted pregnancy. Or? Perhaps she'd been raped?" Shaking her head, she whispered, "I would *never* want to carry a child of rape. I couldn't do it, either, if that is what happened to her." She sighed and smiled brokenly. "And I'll never know what caused her to give me away, but I have a far more mature view of it now than when I was a lot younger."

Ram sighed. "And she gave you to a fire department she knew would take you in, feed you and take care of you. She put you in the safest possible place, so I'm sure she loved you enough to do that."

"All those things." She gave him a thoughtful look. "We all have to wrestle with bad things that happen to us, and it takes whatever amount of time to work through it."

"You've helped me so much," he began in a halting, roughened tone. "I laid awake last night for a little while, with you in my arms on the couch while you slept against me, and I could literally feel that ugly hatred dissolving within me, Dare." There was awe in his tone. "You are my gift. I hope you know that…"

She smiled softly and set the cup on the nightstand. "I believe it's the love we've held for so long in our hearts for one another, Ram. Don't you?"

"I believe that now. But I wasn't there until last night. This morning, I feel so much lighter, cleaner inside, thanks to you…"

"Oh, no," she said, "you were ready to release your grief and hatred, Ram. It was your time to make that change on every level, and you trusted yourself this time, and did just that. I'm so happy for you. For us."

He sat there for a long time, thinking, the silence falling softly between them. Finally, he managed, "I believe the love I have for you gave me the trust I needed in order to start the long process of dealing with all this darkness that has lived inside me."

"I agree," she whispered gently. "We had four years, off and on, with one another, Ram, and we both held our love for one another at bay. We couldn't have released it due to the circumstances we were in. We were both mature beyond our years in knowing why it had to be kept a deep secret and we silently, without the other person knowing about it, carry within each of us."

His brows fell and he rested the cup on his thigh. "We'll still have to keep our secret going forward, Dare."

Nodding, she said, "At least we'll carry it together, and for me, that means the world. I feel infused with such happiness that I can barely stand it."

"We're good secret holders," he agreed, his tone becoming more hopeful sounding. "Maybe too good? If command gets wind of our relationship, they'll yank you out of my team in a heartbeat. They won't allow it to get in the way of combat and mission priorities."

She slid off the bed, set the cup on the nightstand and walked across the rug, sitting down, facing him, her hands resting on his thighs. "I know that. If we can do it for two years of combat in Afghanistan, then two more years apart, we have the ability to hide it going forward, too."

Reaching out, he smoothed her hair, relishing being able to touch her. "You're right. Not even Adam can know. We have to pretend I'm staying here only because of that one-hour drive to my home in the village. That we're still the same people as before."

"Roger that. For sure."

He placed the cup on the small table nearby. Leaning over, he kissed the top of her head and then he cupped her face. "But we will know. We're in tune with one another." He eased her chin upward as his mouth descended upon hers, tasting her, giving her the love he held so deeply for her for so long.

FOR ONCE, Dare did not want to put on her winter fatigues and pull on her polished black combat boots and get ready for another long day with the medical unit training. Ram was out in the kitchen, loading the dishwasher. At least she would be near Ram because he and the leaders of the Black Wolf ops teams would be deep into strategy and tactics sessions with their commanders, learning the ins and outs of how to go about attacking the Russians. First, she was glad her job was medical, and secondly, that she was an expert on setting up field hospitals. She glanced out the living room windows, the day dawning at 0700. The November sky was a light blue, and she could see sunlight touching the very tops of some of the tallest apartment buildings in downtown Kyiv.

Pulling on her boots and then tying them, she got up and went out to the kitchen, where she could smell some wonderful scents of food calling to her. She was starved. Last night was such a powerful, emotional moment for both of them. Ram looked amazingly better this morning. She would swear even the color of his skin had lightened from unloading all that emotional trauma from within himself.

Dare willingly became the receptacle of his grief and loss, and intuitively her empathetic instincts, which had been finely honed by combat over the years, knew that she was the right person for him to trust and share it with. Love blossomed in her heart and it felt like a wonderful, warm blanket flowing across her chest, making her feel as if walking on air and not on the floor. Almost giddy with joy, she met and held his intense gaze that radiated his love for her. It took her breath away. She smiled, feeling like ten thousand suns were radiating from her heart toward his. They had loved one another for so long…so long…and now, it was here. Right now. She walked into the kitchen.

Reaching upward, sliding her arms around his shoulders, she met his mouth, cherishing his lips, his moist breath flowing across her cheek. Closing her eyes, she drowned in his masculinity and strength, which he held in check, sharing only his tender, loving side with her to absorb and glory within. That outer strength that was always like a powerful shield was still present, but now, it embraced both of them. She wanted to share so much more with him, but time wasn't on their side, and she deepened the kiss, infusing him with so much of her love that she held for him alone. Slowly, they separated and they opened their eyes. Dare moved her fingers through his dark hair, giving him a trembling smile.

"I could do this all day with you," she whispered, their noses almost touching.

"Me, too," he growled. Raising his head, he rasped, "But not right now. We have to be at our respective meetings."

Groaning, she nodded, wanting to keep her hands around him, feeling the thick muscles in his back tighten. He wrapped his arm around her waist, bringing her against him, pressing a kiss into her tousled hair. "Tonight?"

She reached up, caressing his cheek. "Tonight."

"We need some fuel for today."

"I'm hungry," she admitted, stopping a few feet away from him.

"Breakfast will be ready shortly," he promised, giving her a swift, hard kiss and then releasing her.

Chapter Eight

December 1

Dare gave Ram an apologetic look as she entered her apartment. She'd spent an hour across the hallway with Adam's family. She hadn't been sure when Ram would arrive home. The word *home* sounded so sweet, so reassuring to her. Darkness had long since fallen over Kyiv, and she had another full day of training with field hospitals. He was padding across the living room, a towel across his naked shoulders and another wrapped around his waist, having just come from a shower, his flesh gleaming.

"Sorry I'm late," she offered. Despite her lateness, she could appreciate that he was eye candy of the best kind.

He halted and nodded. "I just got home myself. Chaotic days now."

Shutting the door, she made a face. "Things are heating up, for sure," she said, walking toward him. "I've waited all day for this moment." She dropped her canvas medical bag on the floor and placed her arms around his broad shoulders. The glitter in his eyes made her smile as he pulled her possessively against him. "You look like you're on the hunt," she teased, absorbing his long fingers moving gently across her shoulders, chasing the tension in them away.

"Let's shut out the real world for a while," he growled, leaning down, kissing her, pressing her fully against him.

Making a humming sound of agreement, she relaxed in his grip. With their schedules, which never agreed, the ten-to-sixteen-hour days, they were usually exhausted by the time they arrived at her apartment. But tonight, it was different. She met his mouth with equal relish, her arms tightening around his shoulders. Hunger for him surged through her. His hand running down the length of her spine, cupping her hips, bringing her solidly against him left no question he wanted her. Gradually, they parted and she studied his narrowed gaze upon her.

"Let me take a shower? I'm hungry, but not for food right now. How about you?"

He eased her away from him, giving her a rueful grin. "Is tonight the night? Finally?"

She laughed a little. "I can't stand it anymore," she admitted.

"Same here," he said, releasing her. "Get your shower. I'll see you in the bedroom. I'm not sleeping alone anymore, Dare. You okay with that?"

"More than okay with it. It's just our schedules, Ram, that's all. I'll see you in about thirty minutes…" And she made her way down the hall to the bathroom.

Turning, he padded across the room, locking the

front door. The drapes were already drawn closed across the bank of windows that faced the highway. He wasn't sure who was more starved for the other: Dare or himself.

Ram had held off sleeping with her because he knew how precious sleep was right now for both of them. They'd agreed to wait until a more opportune time, a less demanding time so that they could have some private moments together.

He was waiting in her bed when she came in, a towel wrapped around her. With only one small light on, she appeared out of the darkness of the hall, more magic than real to him. "Feel better?"

She sat on the edge of the bed, removing the towel, naked. "I feel cleaner, for sure. Today was brutal. When I got home earlier, Lera caught me coming in and said Anna had slipped and fallen on a patch of ice coming home from the school bus stop. Could I come over and look at her swollen ankle? She had sprained it. I'm sorry I wasn't here when you got home."

He gazed up at her lean, tightly muscled body, appreciating her beauty, the soft light emphasizing her rounding curves that were naturally hers. Reaching out, he caressed her waist and hip. "You did the right thing. I just figured you were running late as usual."

"I wanted tonight to be ours, Ram. I really did. But real life happens."

"Is Anna okay now?"

"Yes. I wrapped her ankle in an Ace bandage and Lera will soak it in arnica-herbed warm water a couple of times tonight before she goes to bed. That will help reduce the swelling. It hurts her a lot tonight, but in a week or two, she'll be good as new."

"I'm glad you were there for them." He looked up at her as she finished drying her damp hair. "You are always there for so many people, Dare."

She placed the towel on the nearby rocking chair and turned, moving to where he lay in the center of the bed, leaning down and kissing him. "I want to be there for you...for us..."

He nodded, seeing the frustration in her expression. "Tonight? This is special for us, Dare," he rasped, getting her settled next to him, parallel to where he lay. He slid his fingers through her damp strands, smoothing them away from her face. "Tonight is ours...no matter what lies ahead for all of us." He held her luminous gaze. "Do you know how many years I've dreamed of this? How many dreams I've had of kissing you? Making love with you?"

She barely shook her head, lost in the warmth of his burning gaze, his utter vulnerability being openly shared with her. Her heart mushroomed with so much joy.

Leaning over, he coaxed her lips open so that he could fully curve and fit his mouth against hers. Ram felt Dare sigh, as if she'd waited a lifetime for this moment. He slipped his arm around her, anchoring her more securely against him, and moved his other hand beneath her neck and head, angling her more surely so he could take full advantage of her pliant willingness. As he moved his tongue to first one corner of her mouth and then the other, he felt her react, arching innocently against him. A quiver of pleasure thrummed through her and he felt utter satisfaction, allowing her to set their pace. He settled her beneath him.

Ram knew Dare was wet. She was more than ready. It was torture to not engage more with her. She pressed against him, breasts teasing his taut chest, her fingers digging deep into the muscles of his bunched shoulders, signaling she wanted a lot more than just his kiss.

Damp strands of hair clung to her temple where he followed her hairline with tender kisses. She nuzzled beneath his jaw, caressing his chest as he kept most of his weight off her. Ram was reverent toward Dare, kissing her brow, her nose, her flushed cheek and, finally, her lips once more. There was such unparalleled love within Dare as she met his mouth, kissing him deeply and sharing their uneven breaths with one another.

Ram's mind was melting. He rolled on a condom. He ached like fire itself, his body begging for release. Dare's mouth was beguiling, her kisses sensual and filled with knowing. Ram knew she was lost in the heat of their contact. Hell, he wanted to be, too, but one of them had to keep their brain online at least for a little while longer. As her lips hungrily met his, more demanding, needy, Ram groaned. The tempo changed because her mouth was wreaking sizzling heat straight down to his lower body. In agony of another sort, Ram shifted his weight to both his elbows on either side of her head and lifted his hands, gently framing her face once more.

Sharing a fiery, molten kiss with one another.

After easing beside her, he brushed his tongue

against the peaks of her nipples, and he heard her whimper, thrusting her pelvis against him. Ram slid his hand down across it, following the taut, satin curve of her thigh, and slowly opened her to him. He heard Dare moan, as if anticipating his coming caresses. It was a good sign, and he began to lick and kiss his way down across her soft, rounded belly. Moving over her, their bodies seated with one another, he opened her more, nudging with his knee, wanting to thrust into her sweet, warm body.

He placed his forearms as a frame around her head and rasped, "Look at me…" Her eyes opened and he saw the hunger and need for him in them. "I'm going to go easy, Dare. I don't want to hurt you…"

She nodded. "I want you, Ram…all of you. Don't be afraid. I need you…this…so badly…"

Kissing her parted lips, he whispered, "This moment is for both of us, sweetheart…" He took his time, feeling her wetness, the urgency in calling out his name, and pulling him into her. He allowed her to set the pace and with every slow thrust, it felt as if his mind were melting to the point where he could barely hold on, barely think.

He engaged that swollen knot at her entrance. She was so ripe, so ready. They both had a lot of stored sexual energy and he was going to relieve her first. Ram leaned over, feeling her close to coming, and caught one of her nipples between his teeth and gently squeezed.

A hoarse cry tore from her as he moved more deeply inside her. The explosive power of the orgasm tore through her so swiftly that she nearly lost consciousness as he prolonged the pleasure for her, milking her willing, hungry body. Dare went utterly limp, her breathing chaotic, her lips parted, eyes tightly shut, off in another world of heat and raw, continuous and gratifying sensations.

After each rush of pleasure, he continued to caress and love her with his kisses, moving teasingly to give her more. His ironclad will had kept him in check, but finally, mercifully, he felt that lightning-like bolt of heat plunge down his spinal column and that raw heat bursting out of him, making him growl with utter satisfaction. He held her tight, frozen with the gift his own body was giving him for having the patience to bring her to the same point of utter bliss.

Afterward, he eased out of her and moved to her side, holding her tightly, inhaling her wonderful fragrance, feeling her arms weakly embracing him, face buried against his sweaty neck. Everything was perfect, each feeling heady, light and semiconscious from the deep pleasure they both gave and enjoyed with one another.

Love overwhelmed him and he threaded his long, scarred fingers through her drying hair, kissing her brow, her cheek, wanting to love her like this for the rest of his life. As he held her against him, her breathing slowed down, and so did his. After the raw release and pleasure came the drowsiness and Ram knew just how tired they really were. Dare had fallen asleep in his arms, her breath now soft and slow. Very soon, closing his eyes, with her tucked up against him, feeling so very protective of her, Ram sank into an abyss of darkness that felt as if both of them were in a nest of sorts, alive, safe and happy.

December 2

RAM WAS THE first to awake. He saw sunlight squeezing between the curtains and the window here and there. Losing track of time, he relaxed because this was a rare day off for both of them. Dare was still sleeping and he understood just how brutally exhausted she had become, and how much she had pushed herself in the last three weeks. She wasn't a machine. She was a human, and he knew from rich experience that they might get away with a hard, extreme push every once in a while, but their bodies would buckle under the weight of the strain and they would sleep twelve hours a day for several days in a row.

He moved his hand lightly down her back, her arm across his torso. Her head rested against his shoulder and neck, and he hungrily absorbed the warmth that was her. Lifting his hand, he made sure the blankets and sheet were well in place to keep her warm. He didn't want to get up. He wanted to memorize this night, and this morning after, as no other.

Ram knew what was coming and he didn't fool himself that they would get any time alone, much less to love one another, once the war began. It was going to be a brutal campaign with no relief, no down-time, no going back to the rear for a rest, much less R & R. Right now, every civilian Ukrainian man and woman was preparing to help those who would be on the front lines.

Dare stirred, muttering incoherently. He couldn't make out what she'd said, feeling her remove her arm from around his waist. He noticed how her thick lashes quivered, coming awake. She was a gift to his heart. He slid his arm beneath her neck and eased her onto her back, positioning himself on her left side, his one leg across hers.

"I want to wake up just like this every morning with you," he rasped, claiming her lips, kissing her gently, feeling her return reaction, her arm gliding over his shoulder and around the thick column of his neck.

"Mmm, so do I." She smiled up into his intense, narrowed eyes. "What time is it?" She lifted her head, trying to see the clock on the dresser opposite their bed.

Twisting his head, he said, "0830. We slept a good, long time." Leaning down, he kissed her wrinkled brow. "Now," he warned gruffly, "we've nowhere to go today, no meetings, no field exercises, no nothing. It's our day off and I want to spend it with you."

Nodding, she licked her lips and blinked several times. "I agree… I really slept hard…"

"We both did," he agreed. Frowning, he asked, "How are you feeling about now?"

She smiled. "Never better."

Relieved, he took a deep breath. "Tell me what you want to do today."

"Can I get some coffee into my bloodstream first?" She laughed softly.

He slowly rose and tucked her back into the blankets. "Stay put," he murmured, "I'll make us some…"

DARE SIPPED HER third cup of coffee in the living room, her legs tucked beneath her, leaning into one corner of the couch. Ram had made coffee, gotten a hot shower, dressed and went to work in the kitchen to make them breakfast. She finally got up, showered, dressed and joined him at the kitchen table. How luxurious it was to have that third cup of coffee with him in the living room. He was like a large male lion in the other corner of the sofa, drinking his coffee, the soft silence of happiness surrounding them. Earlier, he'd drawn back the curtains and snow was once more falling silently from the gray sky. Many people were out and about because it was the Christmas season, some carrying packages and admiring the decorations in the store windows.

"I'm stuffed," Dare admitted, touching her tummy beneath her pink chenille sweater. She had curled up, thick pink socks up to just below her knees, choosing a velvet lavender pair of loose pants.

"Makes two of us. We were pretty starved."

She smiled over the rim of her cup. "Sex starved."

He shook his head. "No…love starved. We loved one another last night. It was a dream come true for both of us."

She nodded. "You're right."

"Are you hungry again?" he teased, grinning.

"No…not yet… I'm completely satisfied, thanks to you."

Quiet fell over them. Ram studied her. She had brushed her hair and allowed it to be loose. In civilian clothes, she looked not only at peace, but happiness was radiating from her, as well. "I was thinking…"

"Uh-oh."

He gave her a partial grin. "The day is ours. What would you like to do with it?"

Sighing, she whispered, "Absolutely nothing, but I love walking in the snow, hearing the crunch of our boots in it…and the churches around the area with their bells pealing. I guess I'm nostalgic about the Christmas season."

"Those sounds always make me feel at peace, too."

She gave him a sad look. "Have you ever celebrated Christmas after your family was killed?"

Shaking his head, he muttered, "I couldn't. It brought back so many happy memories, Dare. I avoided those memories like the plague." He looked up at the ceiling and then held her gaze. "But this time? This year? With you? I want to have Christmas again because you're the greatest gift I've ever had besides my family. You make me feel whole, when I know I'm not. Just getting to hold you, loving you, fulfills me. Last night made me want to cry. A good cry of happiness. You were in my arms, and I was able to love you the way I had dreamed of doing so many times in the past… In some ways, I felt like I was in a Christmas fable and so were you. And we were deliriously happy because we were with one another." He sat up, resting his elbows on his knees, gazing at her. "I never realized the depth of my love for you until last night. I felt turned inside out in the best of ways. I never thought I'd be happy again, but with you in my arms? I felt such an incredible, ongoing joy that flooded me, driving out my darkness, my rage, hatred and grief... It all dissolved. After loving you, I had never felt so light, so damned happy from the inside out that I didn't know what to do with myself."

She studied him, tears swimming in her eyes. "I have to come clean, too, Ram. I feel like we're in a snow globe, in this fairy-tale happy romance and everything is right with the world. I know it's not, but that's how I feel right now. Like you? Loving you, having you within me, us becoming one, sent an incredible ribbon of utter joy through me. I was hoping you could feel it because I wanted to share that with you."

"You did in your own way," he reassured her, his voice thick with emotion. Shaking his head, giving her a rueful look, he added, "We had to wait four years for this moment. Four years..."

"I don't regret it. Look what has happened as a result of it. There's a side to me, Ram, that is the dreamer and the idealist. I didn't know you had fallen in love with me. You never gave me a hint. I thought," and she shrugged, "that it was all me, that it was one-sided."

"I felt the same way, but our military mission stopped it cold."

"What makes you think it won't now?" she asked in a whisper, frowning.

"We're more mature," he said. "We know how to function in combat for the team. We're a unit. We're one. But no one will know what we know."

Rolling her eyes, she managed in a strangled tone, "Our future is so uncertain, Ram..."

"And it wasn't over in Afghanistan?"

She shrugged. "You're the pragmatist. Remember? I'm the dreamer and idealist."

His mouth quirked. "I dream, too, sweetheart. Often. I just didn't let you know about it was all."

"It's nice to know now, Ram," she admitted, wiping the corners of her eyes with her fingers.

"Look, we know life isn't easy, Dare. You were given up by your mother. My entire family was murdered. Is it any wonder that we joined the military and went into another kind of war? That our lives have always been about combat in one sort of mode or another in order to survive?"

Nodding, she whispered, "I've often thought along the same track as you—we've always been in combat one way or another. It's as if our life was written for this...for what's to come early next year."

"We survived Afghanistan," he growled. "Sometime in the future, we will settle down and have a real life together."

"I dream of that." She uncurled herself, set the emptied cup on the coffee table and moved to where he sat. He handed her the cup and she placed it next to hers. She folded one leg beneath her, faced Ram and picked up his hands in hers. "Okay," she said in a low tone, "What if we survive this coming war with Russia? What then? What do you want? How do you see your life afterward with me?"

Ram squeezed her long, beautiful fingers gently.

"I will always see it with you," he murmured, holding her worried gaze.

"But...what does that mean, Ram? Do we build or buy a house? What if the Donbas region goes under Russian rule when it's all over? You can never go home. You can never reclaim your family farm or the land. Do you want children? Or not? I need to know these things because it's going to help me get through this war."

He held her hand a little tighter. "After my family was gone, I had no dream of a future until I met you in Afghanistan. Then, I dared to dream. I saw us married, having a home and two children. All I wanted for you, Dare, is for you to pursue what made you happy. If it isn't children? I can live without them. I want to live with you. I want to share my life with you until the day we die."

"You're serious about children?"

"Yes. And you?" He held her gaze.

"I'm twenty-nine now, Ram. If I'm to have children, I'd like to have two by the time I'm thirty-five. I don't want any more than that because it's so expensive to have them." She looked up toward the windows in thought for a moment and then turned back to him. "I'm not even sure we'll survive this war, Ram. One or both of us could be badly injured or killed and we both know that."

"Yes, it could happen. But we go into combat to keep our country a democracy for everyone's family and children, for our future dreams. Without people like us, it wouldn't happen. But it can destroy our dreams we have for one another, too, if we get wounded or killed. It's the last thing I want, but in war, there are no idealists and dreamers, only realists. If you get injured, I will take care of you. I love you, whether you are whole or not. Whether you can have children or not. Love cannot be destroyed, Dare. My love, my loyalty, is to you."

She dragged in a deep breath and pulled her hands from his, wiping her eyes. "I feel the same about you. If you get wounded? I will be there to support and care for you. You have been a part of my life since Afghanistan and I don't want it any other way. We're both seeing the future the same way."

Reaching out, he caressed her pale cheek. "Sweetheart, I love you. And maybe what I'm going to say will sound idealistic, but I believe we will both survive this coming war in one piece, together. We survived Afghanistan. This will be different in some respects, but in other ways, it will be the same. We have passed our trial by fire and not only have we survived, but we've thrived because of it. Ukraine counts heavily on the Black Wolf regimental teams because we are all blooded and experienced. If anyone has a chance to survive this? It is us, so keep your dreams in your heart, as I will mine. We want the same thing—a home and a family. Nothing is ever more important to us Ukrainians than that…"

"There are no idealists in a fox hole," she reminded him quietly. "Right now, today? I'd like to take this time to have serious, searching and detailed talks with you about us, about what we want in our future and how we see it playing out. I know war is fickle and you can't assume anything with it, that it is constantly changing, and abruptly. But," and she placed her hand over heart, "I need to hear, to share that dream, Ram, with you. I want to hear the details of how much you have dreamed for us that I don't know about yet."

He leaned forward, kissing her gently, hands coming to rest on her shoulders. "I promise you, I have four years of dreams and thoughts and possibilities for us, Dare. Yes, let's take this day to look at everything. We have to. I've already had my will changed to give everything I have or own to you, in case I'm killed in combat."

She gave him a shaken look. "I—I hadn't even thought along those lines yet."

"We're going to hammer out plans for our future now," he rasped, kissing her cheek and releasing her. "It will help us get through whatever the Russians are going to throw at us. It will strengthen us, making our resolve unbreakable, and help us keep our focus so we can help our nation survive it all. By laying out our plans? It gives us hope, sweetheart. Hope for a better future, and a peaceful one. Together. My dream of loving you held me together for four years. Think about that. If I can do that, I can keep my dreams alive within my heart."

Silence blanketed them. Finally, Dare whispered, "I like using today to plan. I like knowing you want a home and a family. I have, for the longest time, wanted my own babies… I've helped birth so many in my career as a medic."

"We'll have them, I promise," Ram said gruffly. "I want you happy. We are a team of equals, Dare. We have always worked off one another's strengths, not our weaknesses, and that is one of our main assets that has allowed us to come up to this moment to admit our love and act upon it. We are a team."

Chapter Nine

December 25

It was near 10:00 p.m. when Ram and Dare left the Vorona family activities for the day. They had dinner and gone to church together, come home and eaten some more before everyone got to open their Christmas gifts. Dare was the one with the iPhone camera, taking lots of photos of the girls, of Lera, Adam and Ram. She had been thrilled that everyone loved their Christmas gifts that they had gotten for the family from the Sophia Plaza Christmas Market days earlier.

The flakes were once again falling and everything from the large windows in her apartment showed the snow piling up alongside the wide, massive six-lane avenue. Streets were clean and passable. Kyiv acted like a good Swiss watch: always on time, neat as a pin and clean.

"Oh!" she said, flopping down on the huge sofa, "I'm tired! Are you, Ram?"

He chuckled and removed his sweater, the T-shirt beneath showing off his broad, well-muscled shoulders and chest. "It was a good day," he agreed, guiding her over to the end of the sofa, his arm coming around her shoulders. "The children loved it."

Sighing happily, she nuzzled against his neck and jaw. "It was so hard to keep my hands off of you, to keep my distance over there with Adam and his family."

"I know," he said, a tinge of regret in his tone. "But," he said, sitting up, "maybe this will make you feel less tired?"

She watched as he stood and walked over to a small drawer in the side table next to her rocking chair. What he pulled out looked like a magazine. "What's that?"

He sat down next to her, giving her a pleased look. "Your Christmas present. Didn't you miss getting something from me when we were over there?"

"Well," she said, sitting up, eyeing the folder beneath his large hand in his lap, "yes, but gosh, we got so many gifts from Adam and Lera."

"I didn't want to spring this one on you at the time and you'll see why. I wasn't trying to be sneaky." He grinned.

She laughed with him. "May I have my present now? Curiosity is killing me."

"Go ahead. Merry Christmas, sweetheart." He handed the present to her.

Frowning, she opened up the folder. Looking at it for a long minute in silence, she finally gasped. "No! You didn't!"

Chuckling, he said, "What?" teasingly, his smile widening as she quickly flipped though the glossy tourist brochure's many pages.

"How did you know this about me?" She gave him a shocked look of disbelief.

"I did a little reconnoitering," he answered slyly. "I asked Lera what was your most ardent dream vacation and she told me that you'd always wanted to go to Forest Castle Spa in the Carpathian Mountains, in southwest Ukraine, near the border with Moldova, to their spa, and to ski, because you loved skiing. I didn't know you skied until she told me just before we moved them from Bucha down here to Kyiv."

Making a happy sound, she stared at him, lips parting. "This says a two-week hotel stay, with spa and skiing all-inclusive! How did you manage to get us two weeks of R & R, Ram? I kept hearing that no one was being granted leave right now."

"I wanted to spend some serious time with you, Dare. I talked to our commander and he relented and gave us the leave. He didn't ask why and I wouldn't have answered him even if he had asked me. Lera told me how much you wished you could get a massage, that it helped your shoulders and back. When she added that you were an avid skier? I began to put a plan together. I know how much you love the mountains. And you know what? I like to ski, too. My other brother, Symon, and I were major skiers growing up."

"There's so much I don't know about you," she whispered, deeply touched as she looked at the lavish five-star hotel room where they would be staying. The place was pricey. And it was at the foot of the beautiful Carpathian Mountains that she loved so much.

"This is another way we can share with one another," he added. "The train tickets and hotel reservation are attached at the end of the brochure. We take the train from Kyiv to Bukovel tomorrow night at 1600. We'll have dinner in their dining car, and there is a reservation for a sleeper car because it's nearly thirteen hours from Kyiv to Lviv, and then from Lviv, down to the resort. We can then have breakfast in the dining car and we'll arrive just in time to start our day together."

She sat back, shaking her head. "I—I didn't expect something like this, Ram." Worried, she muttered, "Two weeks? That's a *lot* of money."

"Don't worry about that," he urged. "I've been saving for a long, long time and it's easy to spend it on you because I have it, and secondly, I *wanted* something special for you, Dare. I want our short time together to mean something…something we can hold on to after this war starts."

"What a beautiful gift you've given to both of us," she whispered, moving through the pages slowly. "I don't know if I'll ever leave the spa. They have twenty different types of massage!" She sighed. "I'll be in heaven…"

He sat back, enjoying her response to his gift. "You can try every one of them. You can have as many types of massage as often as you want."

Giving him a dreamy look, she said, "You really know how to amaze me."

"I hope so," he said, matching her grin. "Lera said you were wishing for a salt peel, whatever that means."

"Oh! It's a lovely way to scrape off the dead skin! It makes your body glow afterward."

"If it makes you happy? I'm all for it."

She peered down at the brochure. "Ohhh, and they have mud baths! Finnish sauna, which I love! That hot and cold water is so good for a person's health and body!"

"She also said you like the hot tub, the Jacuzzi?"

Rolling her eyes, she said, "Yes, I do. All of this is so wonderful." And then she laughed and shook her head. "Aren't you interested in these? Don't you love massages?"

Shrugging, he said, "I've never had a massage, Dare."

"They have partner massages. I'll get an appointment for us. You'll love it!"

"I love you," he murmured, becoming more serious.

She reached over, kissing his cheek. "This is just the best gift you could ever have given me under the circumstances, Ram. Thank you."

"I'm just wondering if I'm going to get you on a pair of skis or not," and he laughed.

"You will...but first, the massages. How good a skier are you, anyway?"

"Well," he deadpanned, "I don't take off on a sheer cliff or a steep run. I'm more of an intermediate cross-country or moderate downhill skier. Besides, I don't want to run into a tree and kill myself by accident before this war starts."

They both laughed, nodding and understanding his sardonic comment.

She reached out, sliding her hand into his. "Thank

you for this wonderful, unexpected gift…" The moment was bittersweet because Dare was already counting the days to when their secret life would end and real life and real-world events would take over instead. Shaking herself internally, she made Ram a silent promise that these next two weeks would be memorable for both of them, in the best of ways. She looked at the train tickets on the last page. Tomorrow, near dark, they would climb aboard one of the fastest, most modern trains in Europe at the main train station in downtown Kyiv. "I feel like Alice in Wonderland," she confided, grinning. "Without the rabbit or the Cheshire cat."

"We don't need craziness," he agreed, pulling her into his embrace, settling her against his body, her head resting on his shoulder, her gaze upon his. "These next fourteen days will probably look and feel like we've stepped into another dimension and into a different world, and left this one with all its problems behind."

"Truly," she said, closing the brochure and setting it on the cushion next to her. Slipping her arm around his torso, she kissed his roughened cheek and inhaled his scent that was more of an aphrodisiac than anything else, stirring her lower body to life. "We're entering a dream world, Ram."

"I'll be your prince if you will be my princess. We'll rule our land together," he teased gently, kissing her hair.

Closing her eyes, she whispered, "I like how you see us…"

December 26

DARE TRIED TO absorb everything all at once. She was completely out of her soldier's duties and now turned into a wide-eyed adult as she looked at the U-shaped, five-story hotel rising above them. They exited a taxi gotten at the train station, baggage taken by handlers after they found out which hotel room they were going to be living in for the next two weeks. Above her, the sky was a bright dark blue with a few errant, fluffy white clouds over the Carpathian mountain range. At 9:00 a.m., the sun was bright and she was glad to be wearing her sunglasses, same as Ram. There were so many groups of people from all over the world coming to this vaunted resort. Ram had told her that the Eastern Carpathian Mountains area was a huge worldwide draw to people who loved the great outdoors, hiking, fishing or, in the winter, skiing, ice-skating and other snow sports.

Inside, they were taken to a special area where they could check in. The huge alcove was richly appointed, expensive and grand looking to Dare. What a change from her life in the military! Ram was dressed in a casual pair of jeans, a white velour long-sleeved shirt that was mostly hidden beneath his black leather jacket he wore over it. She saw the hardness he once wore as a team leader completely dissolve. In its place was the man she discovered on the train ride down here, who was very different, and began to realize how relaxed he was becoming within such a short period. Yes, they both needed this serious break in their lives. Holding his hand, they followed the bellhop to a highly polished brass elevator that was set apart from the other banks. They were taken up to the fifth floor, to the very top of the hotel. As the doors opened, and she stepped into what looked like a very expensive penthouse, she gave Ram a startled look. He said nothing, easing her to one side as the bellhop brought in their luggage, placed it in the bedroom and then left.

"Ram," she breathed, looking around at the designer penthouse, "you didn't say we were staying *here*." Giving him a confused look, she knew the design and well-appointed place was for the rich and famous. They were neither.

"I wanted the best for us," he explained, catching her hand, leading her deeper into the huge apartment. Rows of windows allowed sunlight to cascade in, with light gray and maroon curtains that could be pulled shut or opened at a press of a remote button that sat on a glass coffee table in the middle of the living room area. There were huge, colorful bouquets of flowers here and there in very pricey-looking vases. The floor was made of a rich golden-colored hardwood, polished, with a number of well-placed area rugs.

There was a huge kitchen with everything they could ever need or want. Looking into the refrigerator, she saw it was stocked with food, wine, beer and snacks. They would want for nothing. Dare counted at least four large flat-screen TVs in the penthouse. Mentally, she estimated it was at least twenty-five hundred square feet of room. There were two bedrooms, both with king-size beds, each one with a plush white carpet and two master bathrooms to complete them. The shower could easily hold two people at once. The bathtubs were not only large but had Jacuzzi jets so that it would be like receiving a mini-massage. The place was immaculate, beautiful, and she turned to him. "You weren't kidding when you said this was going to be like Alice in Wonderland."

He chuckled, leading down toward the other end. "It has everything," he promised. Stopping, he opened the wooden door. It was a dry sauna. There were thick Turkish towels sitting on the benches just outside the door, just waiting to be utilized.

"When Lera told me how much you loved saunas, I knew that I would get you the penthouse. It is the only room that has one. There are a number of them down in the spa area, but here, you can step into it any time you want."

"And I can take a cold shower afterwards." Dare nodded, smiling up at him. "You've thought of everything." She saw him become pensive and serious. "What are you thinking about, Ram?"

"Us. Like we're stepping out of hell and into heaven for a little while." He squeezed her hand. "I wish I could give this to you as a wedding present. That we could live here forever."

Sliding her arm around his waist, she leaned her head against his shoulder. "I wish that, too, but we know different."

Nodding, he held her close, giving her a squeeze and a kiss on top of her head. "Well, for two weeks, we will pretend, and we will enjoy our time together."

Turning, he said, "Did you see the champagne in the bucket? The two glasses beside it?"

"Yes, I saw it. I've never tasted champagne. Have you?"

"No. I'm a beer kind of guy."

Giggling, she reached up, kissing his cheek.

Looking out of the bank of windows toward the snow-covered Carpathian Mountains, he asked, "What would you like to do first?"

"See the spa?" She grinned. "I really need two or three days of being pampered first. It will help me ramp down."

Nodding, he led her back to the living room, where there was a personal elevator exclusively for the penthouse. "The spa is underground. Let's go reconnoiter. Shall we?"

December 30

THE AIR WAS FRIGID, about thirty degrees, as Dare took off on a ski trail, with Ram not far behind for a day of cross-country skiing. It was ten o'clock in the morning and there were numerous trails all over the highest mountain, nearly six thousand feet, for them to explore at their own leisure. Ram enjoyed cross-country skiing so today the red knapsack he wore on his back contained two thermoses of hot chocolate, along with a lunch, for when they chose to stop and eat at a mineral and hot springs chalet halfway up the mountain. It was quite a climb to get to it, traversing a gentle two-thousand-foot slope and, sometimes, challenging cliff areas that were to be avoided at all costs. Staying on the trail, according to the map of the area, was very necessary.

Many of the groves of evergreens were Scotch pine. Several thousand feet on the slope below were oak, beech, hornbeam and ash trees, all deciduous and barren looking for the winter. Fir trees grew in thick, richly colored green copses here and there, mostly replaced by spruce. There were fifteen types of coniferous trees and Dare couldn't begin to identify all of them. Ram knew most by name, and she was impressed with his botany knowledge. The forests took up one-third of the country. Dare knew there was a thriving timber export business within Ukraine, as well.

Many other people were out this morning on other, intersecting trails that ranged from beginner to easy, moderate and challenging. Ram would stop with Dare when they were going to climb a particularly risky area where the lava cliff faces were located close to the main track.

Cross-country skiing was very popular, Dare was discovering. Whole families would pass by them. Children that were seven or eight years old had skis on and were sliding along with older members of the family. The crisp air invigorated her as she rhythmically moved on her skis. There was no wind at this altitude so far, the day clear and the sky an azure blue in the morning light.

The deep shadows of the Scotch and spruce evergreens brought moments of cooler air as they passed by the thick groves, but then they would pop out onto a slope filled with sunshine and warm up again. The concierge at their hotel had been deeply knowledgeable of the trail systems and Ram had sat with him to map out the day's events with him earlier. After getting the information, they packed their lunch, the thermoses and several bottles of the famous Carpathian mineral water that welled up through the mountain fissures, plus protein bars. The water was well-known and desired by people who visited the spa, the spring unpolluted and coming from the depths of the basalt that had created these mountains millions of years earlier.

Ahead was a steeper slope and Dare saw a family of three disappearing over the top of it. Ram had warned her that there was a steep drop-off on the other side of the coming hill, that it could be dangerous. It was a cliff area, a two-hundred-foot drop composed of black lava, covered with ice and snow very near the trail. And if someone got off the trail, they might not see the dangerous drop beneath the snowpack, and they could go over that cliff without even realizing it was there. Ram had pointed it out on the well-prepared cross-country skiing map he had gotten the evening before.

Looking over her shoulder, she called, "Hey, we're almost halfway there!" They had another thousand feet to go. The springs and heated thermal pools were located at the top of this mountain along with a chalet restaurant. Dare strengthened her stride, in a hurry to get there. It would be a dreamy noontime destination and a well-earned five-star lunch!

Just as she crested the hill, she heard a woman down

below it, screaming. Her attention was to the left, near that cliff. She saw a young boy, perhaps nine years old, on his cross-country skis going over the edge of it. The father was halfway to the boy, slipping, falling, arms outstretched, nearly touching his son's black nylon jacket, but missing him by inches.

Too late!

Dare gasped and yelled over her shoulder, "Ram! A boy has just fallen over that cliff!"

Instantly, he reacted, swiftly moving forward on his skis.

The mother was screaming hysterically, her hands against her mouth, watching her husband sliding down the slope toward the cliff where his son had already disappeared over the lip of it.

No!

Ram leaped to her left, skiing hard to stop the father from going over the cliff.

Dare halted, watching in horror, a cry jammed in her throat.

Ram was able to grab onto one of the long skis, landing hard on his side, his own skis going upward as he rolled onto his back, his gloved hand gripping the end of the man's right ski.

Terrorized, Dare watched as Ram's incredible strength stopped the skier from going over the edge, snow flying in all directions, some of the dangerous black-lava-sharpened rocks revealed.

Gasping, Dare halted, leaned down and released the clamps around her boots, freeing her skis. Leaping forward, sinking halfway up her lower leg, she grabbed at Ram's other hand, hauling back with all her strength to stop both of them from inching toward the edge. Landing with an "omph" on her butt, she halted the men. Once stopped, she released Ram's glove, leaped up and lunged past him, gripping the stranger's flailing gloved hand. He looked like a turtle on his back, unable to flip over, the cross-country skis jammed and not allowing him to move at all. Ram continued to keep his grip on the one ski to ensure he didn't slip over the cliff.

Her breath came in huge spurts as she awkwardly made her way to him, speaking in Ukrainian. The man couldn't be more than in his late twenties or early thirties, terrified, asking her for help. She managed to get his boots released from his skis and then she turned him around as he grabbed both her hands and she hauled him to his feet and away from the cliff face. She saw Ram turn over, releasing his skis as well, and quickly getting to his booted feet.

"Dare!" Ram called, taking the man's other arm. "Slide on your belly toward the edge of the cliff! See if you can spot the boy."

Nodding, she instantly lay down on her belly, hauling herself forward, her gloves in contact with the snow and the basalt beneath it. What she didn't want to do was go over the edge, keeping the toes of her sturdy boots dug downward so she didn't slide forward unless she wanted to. The snow wasn't that deep here, her boots acting as brakes as she inched toward the edge of the cliff hidden by the snow. Below, she saw the boy lying unconscious on a small snow-covered

ledge of black basalt rock. Below that was at least a
150-foot drop to the snow-clad hill below it.

Her combat senses took over. It was automatic for
her to push her emotional reaction downward in order
to study the situation through a medic's eyes as she
breathed hard, white wisps jetting out of her opened
mouth. Behind her, she heard the woman screaming,
"Tymur! Tymur!" and she knew it must be the name
of their son.

Ram was speaking to them, so she focused on the
unmoving boy. Twenty feet down on the cliff face, she
saw a large, thick bush, now barren of leaves, sticking
out of it. Cursing softly, she saw the boy had clipped
it as he fell. A limb the size of her wrist had snapped
off. Her gaze moved to the son. Had the limb gone
through him? She didn't see the whereabouts of it anywhere in the pristine snow patches on that ledge. Either it had snapped off and missed the ledge, plunging
straight down to the bottom, or the limb was partly
hidden somewhere beneath the boy's body.

Blood. She saw it begin to stain the white snow
on his left leg just above his knee. The boy's position made it impossible to see more of his leg from
where she lay.

She got to her hands and knees, jerking a look up
the hill. Ram stood with the couple, his gaze intently
upon her. "Ram! I need that rope from your pack!"

He shrugged out of his pack, swiftly opening it.

To her relief, Dare saw that he had also taken out
the satellite phone that was with him everywhere he
went because he was a Black Wolf team leader. Out

came the rope. He slogged his way down the slope toward her.

"What's the condition of the boy?"

"Blood on his lower right thigh. Might be a femoral artery injury. He clipped a bush on the way down. And a possible head injury. He's unconscious." She grabbed one end of the rope. "Can you call for help?"

"Doing it now." He tapped in some numbers, holding the sat phone to his ear.

Dare saw the couple, both crying, stressed, holding on to one another, nearly hysterical with terror. She was sure that Ram ordered them to stay right where they were and not come any closer to the edge of this cliff. Turning, she crawled back to the rim, pulling the nylon two-inch rope and hurling it over the edge. Urgency thrummed through her as she saw the faint sign of blood growing marginally larger around the child's leg. Now, she was sure it was a femoral injury. The boy, depending upon how bad the artery had been torn open, could bleed to death in a minute or less. If she was lucky, the artery got punctured but not fully torn open. He'd bleed out, just not as fast, if that was true. It might give her the time to get down there and save his life. Her heart pounding, she saw that there was ten feet of the rope to spare.

Ram came to her side, on his hands and knees after making the call for emergency help.

"I called hotel Rescue. They have a helicopter. I told them what happened." He looked around. "There's nowhere to land around here and I told them to bring a basket that they could wench down from the helo and lower it to the boy."

Rapidly, Dare pulled the rope up. "How soon?" she demanded, handing it to him. She moved back and grabbed her medical pack, placing it on her shoulders and strapping it on.

"Ten to fifteen minutes," he answered, scowling. "The weather is cooperating. There's not a lot of wind today. That works in our favor."

"Roger that. Lower me down there, Ram? That kid isn't going to make it without a tourniquet around his thigh."

Ram understood and looped one end of the rope around her waist, knotting it well so it could not come loose on her descent. He brought the other end up. Dare had been trained for mountain-climbing skills after she joined his team in Afghanistan. They wasted no words, each knowing what the other must do. There was a large pine tree nearby and he looped the other end of the rope around it, snugging and tightening it so that it could not loosen as Dare made her way down the cliff. He went to the edge, gripping the rope. "Ready?"

"Yes."

They were now in complete combat mode. Ram sat down in the snow, using a large, rounded rock to rest his boots against so he could use his weight and leverage to help her get down the cliff safely. Dare was over the cliff, boots against the black lava rock, knees slightly bent while some of the brittle face broke off beneath the weight, falling past her. Gloves around the rope, her focus on the cliff and where she could place her boots, as well as watching the inert child to her left and below her, she made quick work of it. Once on the ledge, testing it, she kept tension on the rope above, unsure if the rock would carry both her and the boy's weight. It seemed to be stable. With the snow on it, she could not tell if there were deep cracks across it or not. That would mean it was unstable. Keeping the rope around her, she shrugged out of the knapsack, dropping it next to the boy, who was pale and lifeless looking.

With a quick check of his vitals, she knew he was unconscious but breathing. Swiftly she checked his legs and saw the red blood staining his left leg just above his knee. There were no broken bones, but his pants had been ripped open and so was his flesh. She saw the leak of blood, a thin spurt with every beat of his heart. Standing, she opened her jacket and jerked off her web belt. She always wore the military belt because it was two inches wide and flat, perfect for a tourniquet. With knowing swiftness, she slid it beneath his upper thigh and began to tighten it.

The child moaned but did not become conscious as she tightened it with precision.

Dare peered down at the gash in his leg, using scissors to slice open the fabric. It was a deep wound. The spurting had slowed considerably due to the application of the tourniquet. Breathing a sigh of relief, she clipped the buckle so that it would stay in that place, cutting off blood supply to that leg. She knew that every ten minutes she'd have to untighten it, allow some blood flow into the leg, or it could create an even worse condition called gangrene, where the boy would lose part or most of his leg as a result. Taking sterile, nonstick gauze from her medical bag, she packed it into the gash until it was filled with it, and then quickly took an Ace bandage from her kit, tightening it around his thin leg so that the pressure of the gauze against the tear in the artery would also act as a wall to block the continued loss of blood. She was aware of nothing else for that moment. Getting the wound wrapped, she grabbed her stethoscope and blood pressure cuff from her knapsack once more. The boy was unmoving and she used one of her gloves beneath his neck to be sure to keep his airway open so he could breathe normally.

She noted that his blood pressure wasn't good, but it had stabilized. He'd lost a lot more blood than she'd first realized. Every second counted now. Dropping the equipment back into the pack, she looked up to see Ram at the edge, silently watching her.

"How long now for the helo?" she yelled, cupping her hands to her mouth.

Ram stood, making another call to Rescue.

Urgency thrummed through Dare. She placed a space blanket around the boy, tightening it so that it wouldn't fall off him and would keep him warm. She glanced at Ram, whose expression was stony. She hurriedly shrugged her medic knapsack over her shoulders and buckled it up.

"Five minutes," he called.

Looking around, she yelled back, "Can that basket be lowered down to here?"

Ram nodded. "Yes, only one tree around. They will have room to maneuver that helo so it shouldn't be a problem getting the basket to that ledge."

That one pine tree kept her tethered and they needed it more than ever now.

The ledge cracked ominously beneath her where she knelt in the snow. Freezing for a moment, she grabbed Tymur, plastering him hard against the front of her body. She yelled to Ram. Too late!

The shelf suddenly gave way.

The rope sang and then jerked.

The air whooshed out of Dare's lungs as she held the boy in a clenching motion tightly against her pendulum-swinging body. She slammed into the cliff, her back taking the bruising force of impact.

She tried to protect her head as her body swung outward once more. Below her, beneath her boots, she wasn't sure she would survive this or not. The child was like a puppet full of sawdust in her arms, unconscious. He couldn't have weighed more than seventy pounds, but it was enough.

"Are you all right?" Ram yelled, cupping his hands to his mouth, watching helplessly as she swung back and forth into the cliff again and again.

"Yes!"

He straightened, calling the helicopter copilot directly on the sat phone. He saw the bright red-and-white helicopter with RESCUE on its side a thousand feet below them, climbing rapidly toward their position. Once in touch with the copilot, he told the woman what had happened. It would matter because there were three people in that craft. The technician on the crane and the wench assembly positioned out the open door would be responsible for getting the large, rectangular metal basket on a steel cable out of the helicopter and down to where Dare was swinging. He went back to the tree to ensure the knot was in place. It was.

The helicopter climbed up and over them, and then slowly came down in altitude, the whapping of the blades becoming thunderous. The blades were whirling at over a hundred miles an hour, the snow blasting off the trees and around the cliff area. Ram remained kneeling, hand on the rope, on the edge of the cliff and watching as the basket began to descend. Would it get entangled with the rope? He watched as it swung slowly around and around, the man at the door, one gloved hand on the wench button, the other on the lip of the bird's open door, looking down, assessing the situation second by second. He could see the technician talking with the pilot as they descended it more. The basket swung side to side. Part of the problem was the blades were sucking up the air and the cliff face was stopping the flow it needed to keep the helo steady and unmoving. It was called "hover out of ground effect," meaning there wasn't enough air around the immediate area to create the lift that the bird needed in order to stay in the air, much less remain in a fixed position. Ram was all too familiar with that issue. If the helo couldn't maintain its altitude integrity? The pilot would have to abandon the basket rescue. Because if he didn't the bird would sink like a rock, striking the nearby cliff and crashing, probably killing everyone on board, not to mention Dare and the unconscious child in her arms.

His heart was in his throat, pulsing and pounding as the basket came nearer and nearer. Dare had stopped swinging and, with one hand around the child's waist, she fumbled and reached for the bottom of the basket as it swung by, trying to stop and stabilize it. He knelt there, frozen, watching and being badly buffeted by the blades whirling fifty feet above him. The roar of the helo and the wind whipped up huge chunks of wet snow. Small to medium tree branches snapped off and slammed into him, nearly knocking him over. He kept his hand on the rope, watching as the basket moved three more feet, some slack in the steel cable. Once there, Dare struggled and maneuvered the best she could to put the child in the basket safely. Ram knew the strength it took to do something like that. Dare made it look easy.

Next, she had to climb in. Moving the basket around to the other side, she threw her long leg up and over the smooth, rounded edge of it, wriggling and hauling herself upward on sheer, brute strength into it. After rolling over, the first thing she did was release the knot in the rope around her waist, throwing it away from the basket.

Ram quickly grabbed the rope that was flying around in the hurricane-force wind. He flattened on the snow once again, watching as the helicopter started to slowly move upward, the basket barely swinging beneath its belly. The pilot eased the bird away from the cliff, desperate to get more air. Ram saw the technician on the wench begin to draw the basket upward on the metal arm that extended outside the door. He watched until, to his utter relief, the man pulled the basket inside to the deck of the helo. He was never so grateful as of this moment.

Grabbing the sat phone, he called the copilot to find out where they were going. There was a hospital not more than five miles from their resort, she told him. She added that three snowmobiles from Rescue were about half a mile away from their position right now, coming fast, to take the three of them down to the parking lot where their cars were at so they could drive to the hospital. Ram thanked the copilot, more than grateful for their swift response and recovery. He hadn't thought about the three of them being left behind and how they were going to get down the hill. He untied the rope from around the pine tree and made his way up to the couple.

"Your son is alive. The woman who cared for him is a combat field surgeon and medic. She's stopped the bleeding on his inner left thigh and they're taking Tymur directly to the closest hospital for treatment. Once we're down in the parking lot, the hospital is only five miles away from there."

The sound of the noisy snowmobiles filled the air. The couple cried with utter relief and joy, seeing them come over the hill toward them. They hugged Ram, thanking him profusely between their tears. Ram hugged them in return and stepped away, putting the sat phone in his pack, along with the lifesaving rope. More than anything else, Dare and the boy were alive. She was probably bruised as hell getting slapped against that cliff again and again, but she would live. And God help him, he loved her even more than ever before. He could have lost her today...but he hadn't. The crisis had been so unexpected, so close...

Chapter Ten

December 30

Dare waited impatiently out in the visitors' lobby of the emergency room area of the hospital. The Moroz family, husband and wife, were on the other side of the automatic doors, with their son, Tymur. She ignored how much her back ached, looking out the large picture windows toward the entrance/exit door to the busy hospital. Her heart skipped with joy as she saw Ram pull into the parking lot. How badly she wanted to see him!

The noonday sunlight was bright and everything looked perfect for a winter day. She smiled as he came through the doors. His face expressed his worry as his gaze locked with hers. Automatically, she stepped forward, opening her arms. In moments, they held one another, and she felt his warmth, the strength and tenderness that Ram shared with her. Pulling back, holding her shoulders, he said, "How is the boy? How are you?"

She managed a slight smile. "The Moroz family is together with a doctor in ER. He's assessing Tymur's condition right now. I'm not family, so I can't go in there and be with them. But I did give the doctor my medical assessment and what I did to help him, and he was grateful for that information."

Nodding, he devoted his attention to her. "What about you? How are you?" He slid his hand from her shoulder down her back, worry in his tone.

Flinching, Dare pulled away, grimacing.

"You're injured?" he demanded.

"It's nothing. I just slammed into that cliff face three times while holding Tymur. I'm going to have some colorful bruises all over my back for the next week, is all. Come on, let's sit down. The husband said he'd let us know the diagnosis on their son. He'll come out and tell us when he knows more."

Hesitating, Ram studied her. "I saw you hit that cliff hard, Dare. You're right—at the very least, you're badly bruised."

She sat down, not resting against the back of the plastic chair. "I'll survive. Come on, sit next to me?"

He sat, picking up her hand and rested it on his thigh. "Did Tymur ever become conscious?"

"Yes, once we were inside the helo. He was scared, didn't know where he was and I wasn't his mother or father. I checked his eyes with a penlight. Both pupils were equal and responsive, which is a good sign. He's suffered a third-class concussion, but the fact his pupils dilated to the light, both of them, tells me that it's a mild one, not severe and not causing a brain bleed. They'll probably scan his brain, just in case. We'll see…"

Dare had worn her dark green heavy winter jacket that hung over her hips. Ram looked at it and saw jagged tears of the fabric all across the back of it. He knew the cutting edge of basalt was as sharp as a skinning knife. Looking at the fabric, he murmured, "Your coat is chewed up but good."

"I'm not surprised, but it did its work. It protected my back from the worst that could have happened. If I hadn't been wearing it, my skin would have been sliced open, or worse, even cut into the muscles of my back."

Ram knew better than to place his hand against her back. "Are you sure you don't want to be checked out by a doctor while we're here?"

"No. What I want…need, is you and I want to climb into that hot tub up in our suite."

"You took heavy physical stress holding Tymur," he rasped, smoothing away some strands of her hair from her temple. "I don't know how you did it. I was scared for you, Dare. When that ledge gave way?" His voice trailed off and he choked up, wrestling with a lot of emotions, unable to speak.

"I'm okay," she whispered, seeing the pain and anxiety in his gaze. "Bruised as hell, but if I get into the hot tub, that water will increase the circulation on my back and actually help reduce the swelling and pain in those areas."

He looked toward the ER doors. "Here's what we're going to do," he said, standing. "I'll go through those doors, find the Moroz family, find out how their son is and then we're going back to the hotel. They can call us and let us know how their son is. I'll leave our phone number with them. Right now? We need to take care of you, too."

RAM WAS HAVING one hell of a time wrestling with updrafts and downdrafts of anxiety and his emotions as he walked Dare into their hotel. She could have died. When the ledge unexpectedly broke beneath her feet, he felt like a knife had ripped out his heart. Despite that, her whole focus had been on grabbing Tymur and holding on to him. He had to keep reminding himself that combat medics in the military think nothing of themselves. Rather, their whole life focus is on their patient, the one they are trying to save from dying. This crisis was no different for her, even though it wasn't a wartime situation. Dare was bred to the bone to serve, to save and, if necessary, give up her life so that the other lived to see their family once again. How close he'd come to losing her today...

Taking the personal penthouse elevator, he saw how strained she'd become. "Is your back bothering you more?" he asked as the doors opened to the penthouse suite.

"A little," she murmured. "It's stiff and cranky is all."

Ram knew it was what she called a "white lie." Her American slang and vernacular had been a two-year education for him when they served in Afghanistan. She would treat herself last, not first. And always, she minimized her own wounds. Only when they would get picked up and flown back to the camp would he find out how bad her injury was. It was no different this time.

The hot tub sat at one end of the large, rectangular master bedroom. He helped her undress and when he saw the extent of the bruising, his stomach clenched.

"Your back looks like a war zone," he muttered unhappily, helping her up the steps and into the tub.

"It feels like a major battle going on right now," she said, managing a one-sided grin. Releasing his steadying hand, she sank into the 104-degree water. Wincing at the water deluging her back, she sighed and closed her eyes. She sat down and was covered up to her shoulders with the swirling, clear mineral spring water. At least the pain should begin to recede because the water contained large amounts of magnesium in it, a natural painkiller.

"Ohhh, this feels so good, Ram."

He stood there, worried. "You've got black, blue, red and purple colors all over your back, Dare."

"Is any of the skin broken?"

He looked closely and shook his head. "No."

"Thank goodness," she said, absorbing the healing heat and water.

"I always carry that salve I shared with you when we were in Afghanistan. It's for bruises and sprains. Do you think it will help your back if I smear some of it on after you get out?" he asked.

"Yes," she murmured, opening her eyes. Reaching out, she touched his arm briefly. "I'm okay, Ram. Don't be upset. Bruises heal fast when they get this kind of attention. And that salve you always carried with you has arnica in it. Remember? It was made by Lera and she always sent the team each a large tin of it about every two months. It's a fabulous herbal salve to treat exactly what I've got."

"It will reduce the swelling, then," he said. "You're lucky you didn't crack or bust a rib the way you two slammed into that cliff face over and over again."

She smiled a little, sluicing water over her face and exposed neck. "That's because Tymur was at least seventy pounds. He was heavy."

"He was over one-third of your weight," he grumbled, scowling. Picking up a white Turkish towel that was thick and fluffy, he placed it on the edge of the hot tub so she could reach it when she was ready to climb out.

"My normal medical pack I carried is fifty pounds. The one I had today was about twenty pounds," she reminded him. "Tymur wasn't the only thing weighting me down."

His cell phone rang and he pulled it out of his back pocket, answering it.

Dare listened. It was Mr. Moroz calling. Ram's dark face lit up, and he actually smiled. When he finished the call, he said, "That was the father. Tymur is in surgery for the torn femoral artery. He said to tell you that the surgeon said you did a good job of stopping the hemorrhaging, that you saved his life. They've stitched up the tear in that artery. You were right, he has a level three concussion, and they ran him through a scan and there is no brain bleed, no fracture of his skull, either. He said they'll keep Tymur in the hospital under observation for three days due to his artery needing to mend after surgery. They want to make sure it's on the way to healing before they release him."

"That's all good news," Dare said, grinning. "Do you know where his parents will stay?"

"They are here at this hotel, but they have been given a family room at the hospital. Once Tymur is out of surgery, they will all be taken there. That way, their son will have his parents nearby and the doctor said it lowers the child's stress levels, and that will help him heal faster and better."

Her smile grew. "That's wonderful. Do they live around here?"

"Kyiv," he said. "A rabbit ran in front of Tymur and he chased it on his cross-country skis and that's how he fell over the cliff. It happened so fast his parents couldn't react in time to grab him and stop him from chasing it."

Shaking her head, she sluiced more water on her face and neck. "He's just a child. He probably thought the rabbit was playing with him and he had absolutely no awareness of that cliff or how treacherous it really was."

"That's what his father just told me. They feel guilty that they let him fall over it."

"They shouldn't. Kids move faster than the speed of light. Plus, they had long skis on and you know how awkward they are to make quick turns with. It's impossible."

"The father said they were not aware of that particular trail and had no information about the trails before they decided to cross-country ski on it. He feels very guilty about it now."

"And that's why they probably weren't more on guard at the time they crested that particular hill," she said, nodding. Brightening, she whispered, "At least this has a happy ending."

Ram nodded, sitting on the side of the hot tub, his feet on the stairs. "I didn't think we would get a happy ending out of this..."

"I saw the terror in your face, Ram. I was scared, too." She took the cloth he handed her. "Those two years with you dissolved my fear. Like you and the rest of the team, I can put my emotions in a box and leave them there. That's what got me and Tymur through that incident."

He nodded, saying nothing, but thinking one helluva lot. This was how it was going to be every day when they had to go to war and stop the Russians from taking Ukraine. He loved her like nothing else in his life. Rubbing his chest, he scowled down at the floor. The awful realization that he was going to struggle much more to not be familiar with Dare in front of the team loomed before him. He knew from experience that Dare lived up to her name: she dared death every day when they were out on a mission. So did the rest of them, but now, admitting his love for her had changed everything. How would he stuff it back into that box deep within himself so it wouldn't end up hurting her or his team?

The common-sense part of him, if this hadn't happened to him but to one of his other team members who had fallen in love with her, would assign Dare to another team. That way, neither of them would be distracted or emotionally color a dangerous situation. Then, they could focus 100 percent on their duties. Distraction caused death. It was that simple.

Afraid that he was the weak link in this conundrum, he intuitively felt Dare could avoid being distracted in her work. But he knew damn well, after today's event, there was no way he could stop the surge of emotions that shattered through him when that ledge dropped out from beneath her and the boy. She hadn't heard him scream her name as he lunged forward to somehow save her, either. And, of course, he couldn't save her, but the drive to do just that overrode his experience and knowledge for a few moments. Love, he decided, had sharp edges to it, and that wasn't always a good thing. Today's unexpected event showed him many things, especially the way he reacted and how Dare was cool, calm, focused and not flummoxed by a bunch of other emotions that might have distracted her. He was the weak link.

That didn't set well with him and he simply had to keep digesting his actions and reactions to those awful moments when he thought she and the boy were going to die. Was there a way out of this? If so, Ram didn't see it. At least…not yet. His chest still roiled with forbidden emotions of losing her, and he rubbed the area of his heart, his scowl deepening. What to do?

DARE MADE A soft sound as she lay naked and stretched out on the massive bed. Ram had drawn up the covers to her waist, sat down next to her hip and began to gently apply the arnica salve over her welts and brightly colored bruises. The hot tub had helped a lot; much of the pain reduced. She shunned taking anything, saying that the arnica would further reduce the swelling by increasing circulation in the area. He was careful to apply it lightly but even then, the reddish-purple areas, in particular, were very sensitive, where deeper impact occurred when she hit that cliff. With each light stroke, he watched her eyelids flutter and, finally, close. Her arms were beneath the pillow that she lay upon. Even though it was midafternoon, Ram knew the whole event had taken a lot out of her. She needed to rest.

After finishing, he could tell that she had dozed off. Shock always made a person sleepy after the initial adrenaline phase of it was over. Leaning down, he brought the sheet and a light blanket up across her shoulders. She didn't stir and that meant she was diving deep into slumber. That was good. How many times after a mission did they all crash and burn back at the camp? After placing the jar of arnica on the bathroom marble ledge next to the washbasin, he washed off his hands. He was tired, too. Even though he wanted to hold her, he knew it wasn't a wise idea right now. What he could do was lie on the bed nearby and that would satisfy his yearning heart and his need to protect her. She'd almost died out there today along with that child. Shaking his head, he dried his hands on a towel and left the bathroom.

As he walked without a sound across the tile floor,

his gaze upon her as she slept deeply, he wanted to touch her hair but refrained. Ram knew how necessary deep sleep was to a person, and of the great healing mechanisms used by a body during that phase. And frankly, he knew he needed to do the same thing. First, he would take a shower and then quietly slip into the bed and join her in sleeping off the day's shock and emotional upset.

Just as he was ready to get into bed, his cell phone vibrated. Scowling, he walked away and shut the bedroom door to take the call.

December 31

MORNING LIGHT PEEKED into the bedroom as Dare slowly became awake. She was warm and lay on her stomach, the pillow gathered around her arms and pressed to her chest. Hearing an odd noise, she turned over and slowly sat up. Her back felt immensely better than it did before. Flicking on a small lamp, she turned to see that the other side of the bed hadn't been slept in. What time was it? Looking at the clock, it was 0800. She'd slept a long time, and, obviously, the shock was responsible for this.

Once she slid off the bed, she eased into a white, fluffy robe that fell to her knees and then slipped into a nearby set of slippers. Rubbing her face, she opened the door. More noise. It sounded like zippers. Curious, she heard it from the other bedroom down the hall. Padding that direction, she saw the door was open. Halting, she noticed their luggage cases lay on the bed and Ram was packing all of them.

"What's going on?" she called, stepping in, her voice rusty.

Looking up, he stopped packing. "I got a call from HQ yesterday evening. Our leave is canceled and they want us back to Kyiv as soon as possible." He walked over to her, studying her intently.

Her heart skipped a beat as he leaned down, kissing her cheek. "There are no trains until 1000 to Lviv and then to Kyiv and I told my CO that."

"What's going on, Ram? Did something happen?" Her voice was low and fraught with worry.

"He wouldn't say."

"But...that's *your* CO, right? Not mine?"

"He's the general over the entire group, Dare. And he said he needed to see both of us as soon as possible." Shrugging, he said, "I'm sorry. I was hoping our time together wouldn't be like this."

She nodded and wrapped her arms around his waist, holding him. "We're on the edge of war. Why should we not expect something like this?"

"You're right," he growled unhappily, kissing her hair. "We have two hours before the train leaves. Why don't you get a shower and change. I'll make us some breakfast."

Releasing him, she nodded. "Okay..."

Ram stood there after she left, feeling terror. He had wanted to use this morning, whenever Dare woke up, to spill out the truth of how he felt about her going to war with him and his team. But it was too late. The terse orders from the general's adjutant last night kept him nearly sleepless and he didn't want to awaken

Dare. She'd needed a good sleep to start her own healing process, so he slept alone, in the other bedroom. He had tossed and turned, wondering if the Russians were already infiltrating their country and their advanced intelligence, thanks to the NATO countries, including the US, were feeding them real-time info along with satellite intel, in order to help them save their country. Had something happened on the ground already?

After finishing the packing, he brought the two pieces of luggage out to the living room. He'd order up some breakfast and have it waiting for Dare when she emerged from her shower. It felt as if the weight and terror of the last twenty-four hours had combined. His shoulders ached with tension. What else could go wrong? They would spend the next thirteen hours on the train, the new year coming in without celebration, but he hadn't been looking forward to it, anyway. They would celebrate New Year's Day by going to Army headquarters and seeing the adjutant, Major Zhuk. So many scenarios crowded into his mind, all bad ones. He'd just found Dare once again, and like a wonderful storybook tale, it was filled with light, joy and love. Now? He felt nothing but internalized anxiety and terror. What was the major going to tell them?

January 1, 2022

At 1500, Ram and Dare were dressed in their camo uniforms and entering the outer office of Major Zhuk, who appeared to be in his early forties. He was a man with a frown on his broad brow, sitting at his large metal desk, strewn with files across the surface of it. Once they had come to attention, he told them, "At ease," and to sit down at the two chairs that had been placed in front of the desk. They did so.

Zhuk opened up a red file, and he devoted his attention to Dare.

"Sergeant Mazur," he began crisply, "the US Army is giving you a field promotion to captain." He handed the paper across the desk to her.

Dare swallowed a gasp, taking the paper. "Sir? What? Why me? I'm a sergeant."

"No longer, Captain Mazur," he said. "As you both know, Ukraine's military forces are working hand in hand with all the NATO countries. I had a brief talk with the head of Medical in your US Army HQ. They said it was necessary to change your designation, but in order for you to take over the coming orders, you had to become an officer. They realized this was quite unusual, but we are in unusual times. Later, when possible, you will be going through the Officer Candidate School in your country, but that won't be very soon. We, the Ukrainian military, are very aware of your important medical and field surgery status and your work with us in Afghanistan. You have spent two years here, in our country, training our medics for field combat duties with brilliant results. We asked your medical branch of the Army to allow us to absorb you temporarily into our Army, to help us with a very specific and immediate task." He handed her another set of papers. "Here are your new orders."

Frowning, Dare took the papers. She bit back a gasp, looked at Ram, and then the major. "You're assigning me here, to HQ in Kyiv, and I'm to take over Logistics on incoming US field hospitals that will be flown here to Ukraine right now? To provide the support they need to get them up and running?"

"Yes," the major said with a crisp nod. "Look at it this way, Captain—you are on loan to us for as long as the war with the Russians last. You are the hub of a very important wheel. Without field hospitals being set up in AOs, areas of operation, close to the battle-fields, to direct the assignment of them, we lack the expertise of the equipment and other supplies coming in from the U.S. We needed an American with Ukrainian language skills to oversee it and you are the perfect person for that important position. You are familiar with field hospitals setup because you are a combat medic. You know about them, how they function and, most important, you know the supplies and what they need. You will be the point person, heading up this very vital area. We want our soldiers to have the best medical field care possible. They deserve this, and your country has been more than willing to provide everything except someone to oversee it. You were the perfect person to stand in that position. Questions?"

Stunned, she held the papers in her lap. "I…well… This means I'm no longer in Captain Kozak's Black Wolf team, then? That I can't be in it or be their team's medic?" She felt her heart tearing open and gave Ram an anxious look. She was unsettled when he looked at her. There was utter relief in his expression. Why relief?

"We've already got a replacement combat medic for his team," the major said briskly. "That aside, do you have any other questions right now? You will be meeting in," he looked at his watch, "one hour with the chief medical officer for the Ukraine Army. I think you will be spending a long night with him. There's a lot of logistics to assimilate. I'm sure you will give him vital information that will help him make the best decisions on field hospitals. You will be his adjutant."

Stunned, she whispered, "No, sir, no other questions." Her throat went dry and she felt as if someone had gut-punched her, the wind out of her lungs temporarily.

Ram scowled and stared at the major. He knew he had to sit and be silent. The major closed Dare's file, placing it in his out-basket. He picked up a blue file with his name on it.

"Captain Kozak, you are being reassigned," the major said. "You will no longer run the team you have. You are being ordered back here, to HQ, to be assigned to the Tactics and Strategy section. You will receive a promotion to major." He handed him a piece of paper. "Congratulations, Major. Further, you will be part of Colonel Marchuk's advanced strategy team and supplying him from your extensive field experience, which is considerable. You will be working here, in HQ, but in another nearby building where our intel people work. Here are your orders." He handed him the set of papers.

Ram took them, stunned speechless as he opened and slowly read them. He'd heard Dare gasp, her hand flying to her lips, her eyes huge with shock. That was how he felt. "Then, sir," he rasped, "you're taking my team away from me? I've been with them since Afghanistan."

"I understand that, Major Kozak. Your team has performed brilliantly and that was due to your remarkable leadership. You are now being rewarded because of it."

"But who is taking over my team?" Ram demanded harshly.

"Your second-in-command, Adam Vorona. He will be receiving a field command and commission to lieutenant, and I will be seeing him in person in an hour. He will assume responsibility for the team. We believe that you had great trust in this man's abilities, is that true?"

Stunned, Ram said, "Yes, sir, I do."

"And, if you were no longer leading your team, that Lieutenant Vorona would be whom you would choose for such a trusted position?"

"Yes, sir, I would. He's as good as I am. The men trust him with their lives. He won't disappoint you or Command."

"Good, we thought the same. Then we are in agreement?"

"Yes, sir," he responded.

"Your familiarity with the US military, their customs, their mindset, as well as working directly with them for the last four years, has led us to conclude that your cross-training and experience is going to help us stop the Russians and win this war that is coming. The US president is fully behind us and they are in the midst of getting us whatever we need to win it. You have a deep understanding and experience with US Army infantrymen, with their black ops groups, which will be your focus here at HQ with Colonel Marchuk's group. You will still be instrumental to the Black Wolf Brigade, Major. Only you will be strategizing with the colonel and his team to keep them at the point of the spear, active and being the first to encounter, engage and stop the Russian tanks."

"Yes, sir, I'm glad I'll still be in the mix with the Black Wolf Brigade."

"You are the right officer to put in this very critical position, Major Kozak. You are to leave here as soon as we are done and go to meet with Colonel Marchuk and his group at his office. My assistant in the other office will give you info on how to get over there."

"Yes, sir. Thank you, sir."

"Questions?" The major looked at both of them. "Your clearances will be above top secret and badges denoting that on your uniforms will be given to you shortly."

Shock rolled through Dare. She had top-secret clearance, but there was another one above that. And few people were given that status.

"My assistant has a set of officer's insignias to put on both your uniforms, Captain Mazur. She'll also get you an officer's clothing allowance, credentials to go to our uniform and supplies depot, and get the rest of whatever you need. That set of papers will get you into the Officer's Store to make the purchases you must have. Even though you are a US citizen, you're also a citizen of Ukraine. You will be wearing Ukrainian uniforms at all times when on duty."

"Yes, sir," she said faintly.

"Major Kozak? Your job starts immediately and they are waiting for you right now. Captain Mazur? You will start your new job tomorrow at 0900, here, in this building. My assistant will have an information packet ready for you once we're finished here. Questions?"

Dare and Ram stood, coming to attention, saying simultaneously, "No, sir," did an about-face and left his office for a brand-new world that had just been handed to them.

January 2

IT WAS 0100 when Ram finally made it back to Dare's apartment. He'd called her two different times, letting her know that he was up to his hocks in a strategic plan that he couldn't leave or discuss, and that it was going to be a long night. Entering the ground-floor apartment, he found Dare in her flannel pajamas and fuzzy, long bathrobe. Her legs were tucked beneath her and he saw she was working on a lot of papers that were spread out around her rocker. She looked up when he entered.

"You're home," she said, setting her papers aside and meeting him halfway across the living room. She placed her arms around his shoulders, and he carefully pulled her to him and they kissed. He smelled of cold, fresh winter air, and she pulled away enough to see the tabs with the major insignia on his shoulders. "Are you in shock? I know I am." She released him and they walked to the couch.

Running his hand through his short hair after dropping his cap on the lamp table, he said, "I didn't see this coming at all."

"Neither did I," she whispered, sitting down next to him. "I'm assuming you were in a serious planning session."

"Yes, and it's top secret." He turned to her, worry in his eyes. "How are you? Your back? Those bruises?"

"I know they're there," she said, smiling slightly. "I think some more arnica on them after you get a shower is in order. Otherwise, I'm fine. I'm just in general shock over this turn of events, Ram."

He sighed and shook his head. "Makes two of us." Holding her warm gaze, he said, "You know what this means, don't you?"

"I think I do, or at least I hope I do." She reached out, sliding her fingers into his. "We are safe, in a manner of speaking. That doesn't mean the Russians aren't going to try and take Kyiv, or that we're safe here because I know we're not. But we're not out on the front lines, either."

He lifted her hand, kissing the back of it. "To tell you the truth, Dare? I'm glad this happened. I was torn up inside by the fact you and I, and our love for one another, must be a secret. Hiding it or pretending it didn't exist in the team bothered the hell out of me. I didn't know what to do," he rasped, holding her gaze. "After what happened with that boy the other day? And how I felt when I thought you were going to fall to your death? I came out of that event realizing that I couldn't put my emotions away when it came to you. I didn't know that until that accident happened."

She compressed her lips and nodded. "We haven't had a chance to really sit down and discuss all of what happened on that day. I was thinking what if that had been you with the boy? That the ledge gave way and I was the one up above, watching it happen and me thinking you were going to fall to your death." She placed her other hand over his. "Ram, you and I came to the same understanding that we couldn't stop our emotions, our worry and anxiety for one another out in the field."

"I didn't know what to do," he admitted again gruffly.

"I was going to come back here and ask my commanding officer to take me out of your team and put me in another one," she said in a low, emotional tone. "I didn't know what else to do, except remove myself from the team. I didn't want to do that, but I couldn't see any other way out of our dilemma."

"Well," he said, drawing in a deep breath, "command did it for us." He managed a sour grin. "What I like about it is that you and I can live here, we can get married now because we're both officers and we're not working together. We can have a home, Dare. A life together. I know it isn't a hundred percent safe here in Kyiv, but it's a lot better than being the tip of the spear in a black ops team."

"I've been thinking about all of that, Ram. The thought of having you safe, probably squirreled away in a basement-level concrete-like bunker with intel people, you are very safe even if missiles or bombs start falling."

Nodding, he said, "You're right. We're three stories belowground and with plenty of escape routes if we do take a hit." He released her hand and drew her gently against him, holding her. "I want you safe. And I know that when a field hospital is set up, it's usually behind the lines, but you're still not that safe."

"I know," she said, sliding her hand across his upper chest. "But I'll be careful. And it's part of my job as I see it to be out where these field hospitals are going up, to ensure correct and proper procedures are being followed."

"It's a lot safer than being with a team," he agreed. "I have to tell you, I'm so relieved you are not going to be on the front lines."

"I saw that in your face the instant the major told me my orders. I could almost read how grateful you were for the sudden twists and turns in our lives."

Turning, he kissed her lips, taking in the honey of who she was, her taste, that fragrance signature that was only her. "I love you," he whispered against her wet lips, looking into her partly opened eyes, seeing her love for him mirrored in them. "Be my wife. Marry me soon? We don't have to hide that we're in love or that we want a life together anymore."

Nodding and lifting her hand, her fingers against

his unshaven cheeks, she whispered, "Let's go to a jeweler and we'll pick out the ring soon."

"I'll make sure it happens."

"We can live here, in this apartment. I'm happy to do that because Lera will need help when Adam leaves with the team. I want to be near Lera and the girls. I can be of help and support to them."

"Yes, to all of that." He eased away. "I'm going to get a shower. Meet me in the bedroom and I'll put the arnica on your bruises for you."

"And then," she said, smiling into his darkening eyes, "I want to celebrate this moment with you, with the turn of our luck and being able to live together as wife and husband. This is the best secret Christmas gift we'll ever receive."

He kissed her gently. "Roger that, sweetheart. We have a war to fight and we're going to win it. It won't be easy, but just knowing that I'm coming home to you every night is a priceless gift that will keep on giving. I love you…"

* * * * *